FURY AT TROON'S FERRY

In the gathering darkness he strode purposefully up the empty street. The only sounds came from the saloon; men's raucous voices and the shrill laughter of women. His wife, Leah, had once said that nothing was achieved by violence . . . But now he was convinced that she was wrong, and his desire was to inflict vengeance. Before bullets started flying, as surely they must, would he be able to extract the truth from the man he sought . . . and despised?

MARK BANNERMAN

FURY AT TROON'S FERRY

Complete and Unabridged

LINFORD
Leicester

First published in Great Britain in 2006 by
Robert Hale Limited
London

First Linford Edition
published 2007
by arrangement with
Robert Hale Limited
London

The moral right of the author
has been asserted

British Library CIP Data

Bannerman, Mark
    Fury at Troon's Ferry.—Large print ed.—
Linford western library
    1. Western stories
    2. Large type books
    I. Title
    823.9'14 [F]

ISBN 978–1–84617–621–0

Published by
F. A. Thorpe (Publishing)
Anstey, Leicestershire

Set by Words & Graphics Ltd.
Anstey, Leicestershire
Printed and bound in Great Britain by
T. J. International Ltd., Padstow, Cornwall

This book is printed on acid-free paper

For my much-appreciated cousin June Bach who always pulls my books out an extra inch on library shelves to tempt borrowers

1

She waited until she could stand its crescendo no longer. She touched her elbow to his ribs, disturbing his slumber. Her body might be rounded with a first child, but her elbow was still sharp.

'Angus,' she whispered, 'stop snoring. Turn on your side.'

'Wasn't snoring,' he argued, only half-awake. 'Must've been the crickets you heard.'

'You were snoring, as God is my witness.'

He reached across and rested the work-roughened palm of his hand on her belly, and beneath his touch he felt the tiny stirring of life. He murmured his satisfaction and turned on to his side.

Here, at their remote ferry-house home, both Leah and Angus had taken to sleeping naked these hot Kansas nights. She said it was sinful, but secretly she liked it, revelling in his caresses and gentle whisperings. He'd said that a little sinfulness did no harm, what they did was their own business, and anyway there was nobody out here to concern themselves about it.

She had smiled, murmured: 'Only God,' but she had not pushed the matter further.

Now, quite without warning, their intimate world was shattered. From the external porch their old collie dog, Jack, raised an alarmed bark.

Then three distinct gunshots sounded, vicious whiplash cracks, coming from the outside meadow. Husband and wife snapped to full alertness and sat up in bed, their patchwork quilt cast aside.

'Who's shooting!' Leah cried.

Angus thumped his feet to the rough floorboards, rising in haste, stumbling beneath the low rafters in the darkness. There was no time to make light. He scrambled across the loft-bedroom, catching his shin on a stool, stifling the curse that rose to his lips. He felt for the ladder-top, got his bare feet on to the rungs, and half-fell into the ground-floor living-room. Apprehension broiled inside him, causing his throat to constrict and his breath to come in rasps.

Who was out there, ripping the night asunder with bullets?

Groping through the gloom, he lifted his Spencer rifle down from its wall pegs, aware of the tremble in his hands. The weapon was a .30 calibre Civil War model, a repeater converted from carbine to rifle. He always ensured it was charged, for fear of Osage Indians or any other unwelcome visitors. He would never rely solely on the cup of Cayenne pepper that Leah kept on the dresser as defence.

Had the gunfire been further away, he might have concluded that it was some lonely hunter blasting off in the woods, but these shots had been too close for that.

He drew back the bolts on the door and, still naked, stumbled outside into the hot night, Leah's concerned: 'Be careful, Angus!' in his ears.

His index finger curled inside the Spencer's trigger-guard; he gazed around at the landscape, silvered by the moon and fringed by black forest. The collie Jack came to his heel, growling, nose raised to sniff for alien scent on the night air. Angus could see the river, the Peigan, its ripples and whirlpools flecked with white glints, giving the dark water an odd frostlike appearance in the August night. The roar of the current was backed by the scratchy rasp of humpbacked crickets in the grass.

His senses sought some scurry of movement, but there was nothing beyond the familiar. The ferry-barge, moored at the small wharf, was as a shadowy hulk, the adjacent cotton-woods stirred only by the breeze. He hurried past the water-trough, around the side of the white-timbered house towards the meadow, passing the hog-pen and the patch where Leah had worked so diligently with neat lines of squash, onions, cabbage and herbs for her remedies. Exactly a week ago some night interloper had trampled everything to pulp, ruined the crop. Who had done it?

And now another intrusion.

Ahead, the meadow, bathed in moonlight and shadow, seemed like a flat lake. It should not have been. At least the up-standing shapes of his Jutland draught-horses, Cain and Abel, should have been visible.

He climbed over the meadow-fence, his nakedness forgotten. A moment later, he discovered that the heavy animals were still in the meadow, but their massive bodies were slumped unmoving on the ground, the smell of fresh blood tainting the air. He dropped to his knees, peered close. Both beasts had been shot in their heads, Abel once, Cain twice. Two old friends who for years had patiently plodded countless miles up and down the towpath, providing the power to pull the ferry-barge across the river, enabling it to fight the swift current. Now they had been callously killed, granting satisfaction only to the deed's perpetrator and the growing swarm of bluebottles already drawn by the carcasses.

★ ★ ★

Angus Troon had been the only child of Scottish immigrants. And he had learned how to ride a horse; how the ferry-barge worked; how to tend farm animals; milk cows and goats. All before other children had learned how to play hopscotch. Sadly, his mother had been stricken with the diphtheria and, despite Doctor Elliot treating her throat with a solution of nitrate of silver, she died. Angus was just fourteen years old. Thereafter, he and his father had worked the ferry together.

Troon's Ferry had been constructed by Angus's father, George, in 1857, following the designs created by the

Scottish engineer Duncan Fey and involving four iron stanchions, set in a square, two on each bank of the river, fifty yards apart. All the stanchions had huge cog-wheels, which were linked by two sets of hawsers, one set to haul the flat-barge across the water, the other to bring it back. The power was provided by the sturdy-legged draught-horses.

The house was built next, shaped like a big wedge of cheese, a strong but simple structure. Of stout timber, it boasted two ground-floor rooms and a kitchen, with a fine porch at the front. From the living-room, a ladder led up to the big loft-bedroom.

Across a yard a barn, a stable and shed were erected.

In 1861, Kansas was granted its statehood and settlers flooded in from far and wide, the government being anxious to populate the land. The ferry was busy, providing a continuous trail north from the town of Pawnee Bend, with access across the Peigan River before it narrowed into the two-mile gauntlet of white-water rapids.

The Civil War years came, and Kansas was aflame with violence and death, but fortunately the conflict swept past Pawnee Bend, leaving it unscathed.

Six years after the death of Angus's mother, with rain drawn on a bullying wind, came the October day when his father George seemed out of sorts. He had left aside his breakfast of corncake and bacon and Angus noted there was a blue tinge to his bearded face. He had suffered shortness of breath recently. But George Troon, full of Gaelic stubbornness, insisted on taking six early-morning travellers across the river — seventy yards wide. With rain growing heavier, he was half-way over when Angus, tending the hawser on the near bank, heard the shrill scream of a woman passenger. Glancing up, he shouted with anguish. His father had toppled from the ferry-barge, falling into the wild current, his head disappearing beneath the surface, but showing again, briefly, some ten yards off. He was being swept towards the rapids, a scant half-mile downstream.

Angus had shown no hesitation. He dived from the bank into the torrent, scarcely noticing its iciness in fear for his father. He allowed himself to be drawn by the immense power of the water, beating it impatiently with his arms for even greater haste, aware that the white smudge of his father's head no longer showed. Behind, he could hear the cries of the people stranded mid-stream on the barge, too afraid to come to his aid.

Still pulled by the current, he glanced around for sight of the old man, but saw nothing beyond the mud-coloured river, puckered here and there into whitecaps as it rushed between the wooded banks. Once father or son was drawn to the rapids, there would be little chance of survival. Angus had always viewed the Peigan as their livelihood, as an old friend. Now he fought it as his bitterest enemy.

His sodden clothing was growing

leaden, constantly dragging him under, ducking his head. Each time, he resurfaced, spluttering, gasping for breath, refusing to be beaten.

And then an apparent miracle occurred. He saw his father's white head, bobbing above the surface barely two yards ahead. Crying out with joy, he made a supreme effort to grab the old man — but missed and was drawn under. When he came up, his father had seen him, was reaching for him in desperation. Their hands linked, fingers entwined in a grip that not even the river would break.

Afterwards, Angus had little recollection of how he dragged his father ashore. All he knew was that time had passed. He had sat sodden in the pelting rain, a gloomy grove of cottonwoods offering little shelter, his spirits plummeted to their lowest ebb. The old man's head was cradled in his lap. Angus was only dimly aware when the travellers from the ferry-barge came hurrying along the bank, having somehow contrived the crossing.

As they reached him, Angus's downward gaze remained on his father. His voice came as a sob. 'Died in my arms . . . just lived long enough to thank me for pulling him out of the river.'

Next day, Doctor Elliot from Pawnee Bend diagnosed that George Troon had died of a combination of heart attack and drowning.

2

Now touching twenty, Angus was hard-bodied and lean, well endowed with broad shoulders and biceps. Six feet tall, he weighed some 195 pounds. He had inherited the softness of his father's Scottish tongue. His high-boned features were tanned. He was considered somewhat dour by his friends, but he was hard-working, bristling with male vigour, and let his sweat speak for him.

In sole charge of the ferry, he took on a local man, Ed Mullins, as assistant. Mullins was about fifty, placid-natured, and blighted by a harelip which gave his face the look of an unmade bed. A cleft palate rendered his speech difficult to comprehend. But he was a reliable, industrious man and proved a good friend to Angus, sometimes staying overnight at the ferry.

Two and a half years went by, business was steady, then another event occurred that was to have a life-changing impact on Angus's future.

One late summer's evening a half-dozen riders arrived at the crossing and demanded to be ferried over. They were a coarse-mouthed and arrogant crowd, with a worn, predatory look about them. Their horses were jaded and slick with lather. As the men dismounted and led their animals on to the flat-barge, they all retained their saddle-bags over their shoulders, saddlebags that looked heavy. This was borne out by the way the barge lay deeper than usual in the river.

As was his custom Angus asked for payment before the crossing was undertaken. 'Fifty cents for pedestrians, fifty cents for horses. Six dollars all told.' He addressed himself to the swarthy man who was obviously the leader of the group. Angus was to remember the face for ever. Pale eyes set deeply beneath hooded lids, peering from a face tanned ebony enough to belong to a Negro. A curling moustache fell in silver-grey waves down into a beard of the same colour. He was wearing a mackinaw that was russet-coloured, giving it the appearance of being stained with blood.

The man unleashed an oath in French: 'Sacrebleu!' expressing unjustified shock at the amount he was being charged, his accent confirming his nationality, but one of his companions said: 'Pay up. I guess you can afford it now!'

The Frenchman silenced the speaker with a withering stare, but he reached into his vest pocket and counted out the fare.

Angus accompanied the party on to the barge and signalled to Mullins to lead the horses along the towpath. As the ropes tightened the big crank-wheels creaked into motion, taking up the strain, easing the flat-barge into the current.

Angus was attending to his duties,

ensuring the hawser ran smoothly. He noticed how one man with dark brooding eyes, braided hair and pock-marked face, had remained with his horse, a black Morgan, and he was smoothing its withers. Then another of his clients caught his attention. The voice came strangely high-pitched and on glancing across Angus realized that its owner was a tall youngster with chipmunk cheeks, probably no more than sixteen. Angus just caught his final words . . . *Beacken's Butte*.

It was the reaction this aroused that focused Angus's attention. A hissed '*Tais toi!*' from the silver-bearded leader, and pointedly disapproving looks from the others. The boy lowered his eyes.

Angus turned away, busying himself with a pulley, feigning complete indifference to anything that had been said. He sensed that he was the target for some hard stares, but he kept his own eyes lowered, hummed a tune and assumed an attitude that implied his thoughts were a thousand miles away. After a moment, he no longer felt himself to be the object of attention. However he was thankful when they reached the opposite bank, the horses were led off and their heavily laden owners heaved themselves into their saddles and rode up the woodland trail, disappearing into the trees.

A storm had been building, and next morning the clouds burst open and spat heavy raindrops, making a drumming sound on the earth.

When old Marshal Ringrose from the town of Pawnee Bend called in, dawn's light was illuminating the eastern skyline. He was accompanied by a posse of some dozen townsmen, all hunched in yellow slickers. Angus greeted them from the porch of his house. The overweight marshal's florid face bore an expression of extreme stress. He removed his hat, shook the rain from it.

'Bank's been robbed,' he growled. 'They looted a fortune in gold. Guess they must've crossed over here. Trouble is the rain's wiped the tracks out.'

'Ay, they did,' Angus confirmed. 'They were only customers so far as I was concerned, paid up their dues and rode off. But they were a rough-looking crowd.'

Ringrose leaned forward in his saddle, easing the weight on his buttocks. 'How many?'

'Six. And their leader was a dark man and sounded French.'

The lawman nodded sagely. 'That was them OK. I know that damned Frenchman. His name's Duquemain, Henri Duquemain. He's wanted for murder and robbery across four states.'

Angus pondered for a moment, then said: 'I heard them mention Beacken's Butte.'

Ringrose perked his ears up.

A posse rider turned to one of his companions, a newcomer to the area and explained, 'That's a mountain twenty miles beyond Oakley Gap.'

'You reckon that's where they was

heading?' the marshal asked.

Angus scratched his jaw. 'Can't be sure, but they looked mighty worried when they figured I'd heard.'

'Well, that'll be the first place to look, I guess,' the lawman said. He glanced at Angus. 'We come over to ask you to ride with us. We need all the able-bodied deputies we can get. Will you come?'

Angus frowned but nodded.

'Then raise your right hand while I swear you in.'

Minutes later Angus informed Mullins of events as he saddled his stocking-footed sorrel, Judas. Afterwards he fetched his Spencer from the house, pulled on an oilskin slicker, mounted up and joined the posse. They crossed over the Peigan on the barge.

* * *

They followed the forest trail through the morning, the rain gaining muscle by the minute. Travelling briskly, their horses raised great sprays of water as they splashed through puddles. They rode via the small township of Oakley Gap, a scattering of shacks with the saloon its most noteworthy establishment. Here the posse paused for refreshment. As they stood around the stove and drank coffee, their clothing steaming, Ringrose questioned the locals regarding strangers passing through during the last day or so, but none had been seen. It seemed that, if they had come this way, the outlaws had bypassed the settlement.

Angus felt decidedly uneasy. He wondered whether heading towards Beacken's Butte was a big mistake. The posse could be heading the wrong way; the mention of the place might have had nothing to do with the direction the outlaws were headed. They might even have mentioned the place to put the law off-track. If so, Marshal Ringrose had swallowed the bait like a hungry mackerel.

In the early afternoon they followed

the trail through meadows of tall bedraggled sunflowers which were now turning to seed. Their horses were lathered and weary. Eventually, the dark hump of Beacken's Butte showed, its flattened summit shrouded in cloud. It was in reality a small mountain, or butte, left standing in an area reduced by erosion. At the beginning of the century it had been used as a landmark for pioneer migrant trains. Angus knew that it concealed a multitude of caves and gulches that were ideal for hideaways.

At the base of Beacken's Butte a creek curved between high-ferned banks. Heavy rain had turned it into a freshet. The surrounding ridges offered good vantage points to see if anybody was coming up the main trail, and Marshal Ringrose suspected that if the outlaws were in residence, they'd have a lookout posted. On the other hand, somebody pointed out, with the rain continuing and pursuit not anticipated, their quarry might be holed up in shelter. This would give the posse the advantage of surprise.

Ringrose called a halt well back from the creek, concealed in cottonwoods, and sent Angus and Nathan Fitzsimmons, the lanky Pawnee Bend undertaker, forward on foot for a scout-see.

Angus and Fitzsimmons crept cautiously through a rain-dripping grove of trees, the leaves showing the yellow of late summer. With their guns at the ready, the two men moved towards the higher ground overlooking the creek. Again, doubts assailed Angus. The outlaws could be a hundred miles away by this time. Alternatively, lead might start to fly at any second. Life could be over and done with in the time it takes a bullet to travel a few feet. Consequently, both men moved with their heads ducked into their shoulders, their eyes darting around. They were sodden, having left their yellow slickers with the main party; these would have made them as obvious as sunshine in a storm.

But they reached the higher ground and it was then, as they crouched against the earth, that they heard the clink of cooking-utensils and the low murmur of voices. They had struck lucky! In a small ravine, half-hidden by a big catclaw bush, they glimpsed the flicker of a campfire, and standing about it was a group of men which Angus immediately recognized as that which had crossed on the ferry the previous evening. Even as they watched, one of the group began stamping the fire out. Angus spotted the boy with the chipmunk cheeks standing back from the others, finishing coffee from a tin cup. Maybe he was still unpopular with his companions. If he'd known that his rash words had drawn pursuit, he would have been looking even more doleful now. The gang's horses were tethered further along. The animals were stirring restlessly, snuffling the air, as if suspecting impending departure, or maybe they sensed the nearness of danger.

Angus and Fitzsimmons exchanged nods, then stealthily back-tracked to where Ringrose and the remainder of the posse were waiting.

3

'Maybe we could wait till night,' somebody suggested, 'catch 'em when they're asleep.'

Angus spoke his mind. 'I don't think they'll be hanging around that long. I somehow got the impression they were planning on moving out soon.'

Ringrose nodded. He wiped rain from his face with the back of his hand. He looked weary and unwell, but he said: 'If they've shared out the loot, they'll most likely scatter. We've got to hit 'em now. We'll split up, half of us get below 'em, the rest cross the creek out o' sight, get above 'em so's they don't hightail over the mountain. We'll hit 'em from two sides.'

Most of the posse nodded their agreement. Angus felt a tingle of fear taking hold of him. He couldn't help but wish there was an experienced gunfighter or two in the posse, but they were all ordinary townsfolk, apart from the marshal himself who was past his best years. He wondered whether, despite the outlaws' apparent carelessness, they had set guards who were now reporting back that they were about to be attacked. He prayed not.

The marshal split them up, sending Angus, Fitz-simmons and another fellow down-creek, there to cross over and get along the far rim, impressing upon them the importance of quiet. Ringrose and the remaining force intended attacking from this side.

Angus led the two around a bend in the creek. They waded across, bracing their legs against the rain-swelled current. Everywhere appeared silent and peaceful, apart from the steady fall of rain. Once over the water they were thankful of the cover provided by the age-gnarled rocks. Stealthily, they clambered upward, holding their weapons up to prevent them clinking against the hard surface. At last they reached a suitable vantage point and gazed down. Thank God they hadn't waited until darkness. Already some of the outlaws were saddling their horses and mounting up in readiness to travel on. Angus and his companions sprawled down on the rocks, hugged their rifles into their shoulders and, at a nod, opened fire. This was the first time Angus had ever fired his Spencer in anger and it gave him an uncomfortable feeling. Simultaneously Ringrose's guns blasted out from the far side.

The outlaws were caught in a crossfire and two fell, their horses rearing in panic. Another was crouched down, obviously hit. The remaining three ran off on foot into the cottonwoods and aspen that fringed the bank.

Realizing that they had achieved their purpose, Angus and his companions scrambled down through the ferns, hollering to Ringrose that they were coming. Meanwhile Ringrose and the remainder had waded the creek, bracing themselves against its flow, firing as they went. The chipmunk-cheeked kid lay dead upon the ground, the back of his head a bloody mess. Two of his companions sprawled motionless close by. Ringrose and one of his deputies disappeared into the trees in pursuit of those who'd run off — and soon the vicious snap of pistol fire erupted.

Excitement was pumping inside Angus; his eardrums thrumming. The acrid taint of gunsmoke came on the rain.

It seemed everything had been too easy to be true. He recharged his Spencer. The sound of shooting had him blundering in Ringrose's wake into the trees.

Almost immediately he stumbled over the crouching Will Gallywed, the deputy who had accompanied the marshal as he'd taken up the chase. He was holding his ribs, blood seeping through his fingers. But he waved

Angus away. 'I'll be all right,' he gasped. 'Bullet just grazed my ribs. I'll get back to the others. You best go and help the marshal.'

Angus hesitated, then nodded and rushed on.

A minute later, he found himself on the edge of a clearing — with a man's bullish back turned towards him. He recognized the straggling silver hair. Angus pulled up, holding his breath. From the far side of the clearing Marshal Ringrose's voice sounded. 'This is Marshal Ringrose. We got you covered, Duquemain. Get your hands raised!'

The man with his back to Angus stiffened. '*Allez*, Marshal,' he called in a deep, French accented voice. 'You 'ave caught us. We give up!' He lifted his hands slightly.

Right then, Angus noticed there was a derringer pistol tucked in the Frenchman's boot.

As Ringrose stepped from the trees, his long-barrelled Navy Colt levelled,

Duquemain jerked into motion, throwing himself to the side, his hand clawing for the derringer. The overweight marshal, more sluggish than he used to be, was caught by the speed of the outlaw. Ringrose fired but missed, the bullet winging past Angus's left ear. Ringrose would have fired again but his gun misfired. Meanwhile Duquemain clambered up, laughing scornfully, raised his derringer and took careful aim, knowing that he had the marshal at his mercy. The lawman braced his rotund body for the bullet.

Angus fired his Spencer from the hip. The bullet took Duquemain in the shoulder, causing the breath to explode from his lungs, pitching him forward, his derringer flying. Ringrose immediately stumbled to him, dropping his considerable weight, knees first, on to him, pinning him down. Angus joined him, recocking the Spencer. Somehow, the marshal fumbled with handcuffs and fastened the wrists of the writhing Frenchman.

'My God, Angus,' Ringrose gasped. 'You saved my skin. I'm sure grateful.'

Angus would have enjoyed his moment of glory had not Duquemain turned, blood pumping from his shoulder. His dark features were grimacing with pain, but he fixed Angus with his stare, hatred blazing from his deep-set eyes.

'One day,' he hissed, 'I will make every man in zis posse pay for what's happened. Especially you, Monsieur Ferryman. You will wish you 'ad not been born!'

His threat, its reptilian menace, made Angus's stomach churn.

★ ★ ★

Records of the events that followed are noted in Pawney Bend's court documents. How the three surviving members of the gang, having recovered sufficiently from their wounds, were placed on trial before the circuit judge, Isaac Marrow. Henri Duquemain was sentenced to ten years in the state prison, lucky to escape the rope, saved only by lack of firm evidence. His second-in-command, Silas Glaswall, and Johnny Kypp, the man with the pock-marked face, each got five years.

Ringrose's posse had been lucky in many ways, particularly in timing their arrival just at the moment when Duquemain had recalled his lookout man in readiness for the gang to continue its flight.

It was unfortunate that the same luck was not to extend into the future life of Angus Troon.

4

For two years following the trial life at the ferry-crossing settled back into its normal routine. In Pawnee Bend Marshal Ringrose took his well-earned retirement, handing his badge over to his younger deputy, Fred Terrill. Most folks gradually forgot about the bank robbery and the subsequent violence, but Angus did not. On lonely nights, he would sometimes awaken sweating with the nightmare in which Henri Duquemain returned to fulfil the awesome act of vengeance he'd promised, his hatred enflamed beyond all natural provocation or reason.

Angus knew that at the ferry, which lacked immediate neighbours, he was highly vulnerable, but he reckoned he had another eight years before Duquemain was let loose.

One Sabbath he left Ed Mullins in

charge at the ferry and rode towards town. Several families of Russian settlers had bought land in the area. So-called sodbusters, they had sweated behind their teams and ploughshares and planted red wheat which had taken to the Kansas soil well. Angus wondered if he might try a field of it on his own land. But today his mind was mostly fixed on attending church. He knew he'd frequented the saloon too much of late, drinking, gambling and falling to temptation at 'the palace of sinful pleasure' which had windows of blood-red glass. He figured his soul needed some attention.

Pawnee Bend sat abreast of the point where two main cattle trails converged. It offered a wide street and a multitude of high-framed, wood-fronted structures. On the outskirts were a few classy residences. The town's only church was a building with shiplap siding. Apart from a tall brick chimney, the church's most notable feature was the Gothic-style, arched window above the entrance door. Steps led up at the front.

At the service Angus knelt and prayed for the departed spirits of his mother and father, prayed that he might be worthy of them. Afterwards the congregation rose and sang two hymns, then the Reverend Havelock stepped into the pulpit and railed against sin and the evils of lustfulness.

But despite his attempt to pay attention Angus felt he was being watched. Glancing to the side he met the blue-eyed gaze of a young woman who smiled and looked away. She was slim, her skin smooth and fair and slightly flushed with the heat. A straw bonnet sat at a rakish angle on her golden head. A blue cotton dress fitted itself closely at neck and shoulders and waist, and she was wearing a heavy crucifix. He thought her immensely pretty. For some reason his body was suddenly tingling, particularly in one department. He could not understand himself. When he dared to sneak another glance in her direction, the sermon was over and the congregation had launched into the closing hymn. She was singing devoutly; he could hear her voice amongst the others, sweet and earnest.

As the Reverend Havelock concluded the service and people dispersed he spotted the girl, clutching her Bible. She went up to the minister and kissed him on the cheek, and realization dawned on him. She must be Leah Havelock, the reverend's daughter, who had been away for some years in San Fransisco. He felt a restlessness surge over him, a frustration, but he returned to Judas, jerked the bridle reins from the hitching-rail and mounted up. He rode homeward in a flurry of confusion.

The last time he had seen Leah Havelock was at the schoolhouse. Her mother had only recently passed away, and he recalled Leah as a pale-faced child, a little shy and very serious. Maybe because she was a minister's daughter the other children tended to stay clear of her and she did not get involved with the sneaky games and smutty backchat that often went on behind the school-marm's back. And when she had gone to San Francisco to stay with her aunt, it seemed natural because she was different from the others. And anyway, it didn't seem right for a father to bring up a daughter single-handed.

But now she was back, and she had blossomed into young womanhood in no uncertain way.

Where previously Angus had been indifferent towards her, he now found she was constantly on his mind. Had the brief smile she had given him been some sort of invitation? No female had ever stirred him in this way, implanted in him a sick longing that he feared might never be assuaged. What had he to offer to a refined young lady like her? Maybe she already had an admirer — maybe she was even promised to some educated fellow who was an example of good God-fearing living, fitting her father's high moral principles. The possibility brought panic to Angus.

How could he be in love when all he had to cling to was the brief smile she had given him? Yet he was. And what did he, a clumsy, occasional drinker, poker-player and whorer, have to offer a person like her? His ways had been the very target of her father's damning words when he had delivered his sermon.

But if, in going to church, he had sought to see the wickedness of his ways, then it had had the desired effect. He vowed that henceforth he would stick closely to the righteous path. But he needed to do more than that. He could certainly attend church again on the following Sabbath, but that meant going an entire week without seeing her. Anything could happen during that time. She might even fall in love with some other local man. There would be, he felt certain, plenty of rich ranchers ready to throw their hats into the ring.

After the next two days, Ed Mullins,

struggling to make his words intelligible despite his cleft palate, upbraided him for not paying attention to his work. He knew this was right. He couldn't eat or sleep for thinking about Leah. He realized how downright lonely, how meaningless, his life was.

So on the Wednesday he drove the wagon into town on pretext of picking up supplies. 'By chance' his sauntering walk took him past the minister's fine white house with its columned porch and double-sash windows. Glancing over the fence he saw the neat garden with its well, and an old white dog asleep on the path. He longed for sight of Leah, but she was nowhere to be seen; the front door was firmly closed, and the windows gazed at him with blank eyes.

He waited as long as he dared, and then wandered back to town bitterly disappointed. Maybe he should have hammered on the door, told the Reverend Havelock that he had fallen for his daughter, and that he was in the process of reforming his ways so as to be in a position to ask for her hand! But he had lacked the courage for that. Furthermore, how could he expect a young woman used to life in San Francisco to be at all interested in a man who lived in a humble dwelling at a remote, out-of-town ferry?

But hope drove him to church again the following Sunday. He was rewarded in a way beyond his wildest dreams. He was in the process of mounting the church steps, other folks all around him, when he felt a touch on his arm and turning, his heart took a flip.

She was smiling at him and in a voice entirely lacking the shyness of her childhood, she said, 'Angus Troon, I'm sorry to hear that you've lost your father, but I heard how hard you tried to save him from the river, how you helped to round up those nasty outlaws and how you saved Marshal Ringrose's life.'

He felt his cheeks tingling. He

opened his mouth to speak but no words came.

Her face was heart-shaped. She looked so feminine, and she smelt faintly of lavender.

At last he managed a nod and a smile. 'How did you get on in San Francisco? Was it better than Pawnee Bend?'

'Oh . . . it was different. But I wanted to come home. This is where I belong, Angus.'

He was touched by the way she remembered his name.

She went on: 'Daddy wants me to go back, to take up a teaching appointment.'

He quickly sought to cover his disappointment. His eyes fell upon the cameo brooch clipped to her dress at the curve of her breast. 'Your brooch is so pretty,' he said.

Sadness clouded her eyes. 'Yes, it belonged to my mother.'

He regretted that he had reminded her of her deceased mother, but before he could speak again, she touched his arm. 'We must go inside. The service is about to begin.'

As they stepped into the church, she said, 'May I sit with you, Angus?'

After the last hymn he nervously enquired if she would walk out with him. She smiled, hesitated, and then bobbed her blonde head.

That afternoon, in the warm spring sunshine, he was relieved to learn that she was not committed to another man. They wandered through meadows and woods, aware of the scent of bluebells. Somehow, this year, the flowers seemed bigger, brighter and sweeter than ever before. Before long her hand slipped into his and their togetherness seemed natural. They started singing 'Rock of Ages' as they walked down the centre of a trail, and they laughed at themselves. She told him that when she had mentioned to her father that they were walking out together, he had said that they should have a chaperon. But she had told him not to talk nonsense.

She had a zest for life. He noticed how it blazed from her eyes, betraying itself in the manner she held her nether lip between her teeth.

'I love Kansas so much, Angus!' she exclaimed. 'I love the air, the rivers, the hills, everything. I longed to come back when I was away.'

Presently they sat on the wall of the truss-bridge, watching silver trout flashing through the water beneath them and Angus had never felt happier in his life. But then he recalled her earlier words.

'Do you think you will go back to San Francisco, Leah?'

She sobered, her brow furrowed, then she said, 'I must go where the Lord guides me.'

When Angus took her home their heads were so close that he could see how her lips and eyelids quivered; she opened her blue eyes full on his, like a lovely wild animal, and then she laughed, said, 'Thanks, Angus,' and turned indoors.

Two days later, he received a pretty card, passed on to him by a traveller who was travelling through. It was from Leah, inviting him to tea on the following Wednesday.

In the subsequent weeks he learned so much about Leah, about the strength of her faith in the Lord and in prayer. He also became better acquainted with her father and found him to be an affable and kind man with a lively humour, and not just the fierce deliverer of fire and brimstone that he appeared in the pulpit.

Gradually Angus sensed something mysterious about Leah, some secret depth that was beyond his reach. Moments when she was quiet and seemed to drift away — but she always returned. Then one day the Reverend Havelock told him how, even from a child, she had had the ability to converse with the Lord, and there was a warmth in her hands that could bring healing.

He also warned Angus that he was

sure the Lord was calling Leah to San Francisco; the teaching post at college awaited her.

'Do you know, my boy,' he went on, 'that the San Francisco Board of Education forbids its teachers to venture into matrimony? They believe that in so doing females place their own feelings above public welfare.'

'That's not fair!' Angus exclaimed.

The reverend did not answer.

Angus's heart sank to his boots, but he did not raise the matter for several weeks with Leah because he feared she might give him an answer he did not wish to hear. Then, at last, he could stand the torment no longer.

'Leah,' he said with trepidation, 'your daddy said you might go to San Francisco to take up that teaching appointment.'

'Oh, I know,' she responded. 'I talked to him about that. I told him I had spoken to the Lord, and He had told me that I wasn't to do that, that I wasn't suited to fancy living. The

Lord told me my duty was to marry you, Angus, and to make you a good wife.'

'The Lord actually knew about me?' he gasped, hoping the Lord hadn't told her too much.

'Sure did,' she said solemnly. 'He mentioned you by name.'

Angus laughed, then he took her in his arms.

He had the suspicion that sometimes Leah manipulated the Lord. Maybe she'd manipulate him too, but he wouldn't care.

The following spring they were married. Leah wore a simple white dress, with a wreath of orange-blossoms as her crown. He wore his new broadcloth suit, white starched shirt and 'French calf' boots. Her father conducted the service, bonding them as one flesh, finishing with the warning: *What therefore God hath joined together, let not man put asunder!*

Following the ceremony, Angus collected their marriage certificate. It bore a 10-cent internal revenue stamp, thus making the marriage valid.

With the simple celebration in Pawnee Bend over, husband and wife returned to the ferry-house and he carried her over the threshold and they kissed, amid riotous laughter, and thus embarked upon their new life together. It wasn't easy, for they both proved feisty by nature. But they each learned the value of laughter, and Leah never once complained about the hardness of life, always finding a quote from the Bible to salve their problems.

Her 'woman's touch' brought the old house to life, reviving memories of the time when his mother had been alive. She made the most wonderful cheese. 'Don't praise me,' she would laugh. 'Mary makes the cheese. That nanny-goat is a true darling!'

In due course she made use of her powers and folks came to the house to benefit from the healing that the warmth of her hands could bring. She hoed the earth, cultivated herbs

— nettles for kidney sickness, buckthorn for unblocking constipation, eucalyptus for colds and a blue herb she gave to women who did not want babies.

And Angus was as happy as a cow in clover, and would have remained so had not the demons of his past reared up, like a deep dark forest, to strangle his contentment.

5

After what could be called nothing less than the 'cold-blooded murder' of the two draught-horses, Angus and Leah were beset with grief not only over the loss of two faithful servants, but over the temporary halt of their business and income. Lack of transport across the river caused great concern amongst local folk, many of whom, in fact, contributed to a fund set up to purchase replacement animals. These were impossible to find locally, but news came, carried by a horseback dentist, that a pair of suitable horses were available at Bear Springs, a town to the south. However, they would require training in pulling the ropes.

Angus, Ed Mullins and the pregnant Leah travelled down to Bear Springs and inspected the animals, which were seven years old. They were muscular

Ardennais, with broad faces and hugely crested necks.

'They'll do us proud,' Leah pronounced.

Within a week the pair were back at the ferry and being subjected to intensive instruction.

Angus had always imagined that he had nothing to fear from Henri Duquemain until the outlaw had served his ten-year sentence, but he realized that five years had elapsed since the trial — and the individuals sentenced with the Frenchman would now have been set free. One of them, he recalled, was the man with the pock-marked face and braided hair — Johnny Kypp. He could not remember much about the other man, apart from the fact that he had a narrow and mean face.

Angus became convinced that the misfortunes he was experiencing were linked to Johnny Kypp's release. Firstly there had been the destruction of Leah's vegetable garden. Then had come the even worse crime of killing the horses and crippling his livelihood. Maybe Kypp was carrying out vengeance on Duquemain's behalf, or maybe he considered he had his own scores to settle and was as full of hatred as was the Frenchman himself.

The prospect left Angus totally depressed.

With Leah close to giving birth, the pain in her back troubling her, coupled with the remoteness of the ferry crossing, he lived with fear, constantly looking over his shoulder, jumping at shadows and listening for unfamiliar sounds at night, unable to relax. He always kept a gun at hand.

The new horses settled in well. During the warm summer nights Angus, Ed Mullins and another hired man took turns to watch over the grazing animals and keep guard generally, but this wasn't something that Angus could afford indefinitely. He strove to believe that whoever was responsible for the crimes had now drifted away, never to return, but the threat remained. Would it ever depart?

As summer faded into fall, the two draught-horses, now fully trained, were locked in the barn at night. Trade at the ferry crossing had resumed. Angus knew that there were still plenty of ways in which he could be victimized.

In October Leah's time came.

'If the cow was expecting,' she said, 'she'd be rested, but a woman has to cook and clean right up to the last minute.'

Angus made a sympathetic sound, but she looked at him and smiled. 'Wouldn't have it any other way,' she said.

The birth was not easy, but she bore it stoically, Angus doing his ham-fisted best to help because the midwife didn't arrive at the ferry house until after the event.

It was Angus who cut the cord, and washed the blood from the tiny body and pronounced a joyful: 'It's a girl — a wee lassie!'

Leah was exhausted, but her blue

eyes were glowing with pride. 'Let's call her Anna, after my mother,' she murmured.

Angus nodded. 'As long as the next one's called after my father.'

'Next one?' she gasped. 'Not yet.'

Following the birth Angus became even more protective. Anna was the apple of her parents' eyes, a child with her mother's fair hair.

The winter of 1886–87 drew in and snow blocked some of the trails, but the swollen, urgent flow of the river prevented its complete freeze. The ferry kept running except for one week when a blizzard closed down everything.

But inside the house they were warm and the baby had brought a new dimension of joy to their lives. She was growing more knowing by the day, their own laughter bringing the first inklings of a smile to her tiny face; her little arms waving all ways.

'One day,' Leah smiled, as she sucked at her breast, 'she'll conduct an orchestra!'

With the weather so severe Angus suspended the overnight guards at the ferry. On several occasions he brought his hogs into the house to save them from freezing.

One night in February he awoke imagining that he heard their old collie Jack howling. He felt a tightening in his throat and with it fear. The dog usually slept in a small shed adjoining the barn. Angus hoped that his barking would carry warning of any night intruders. But now as he lay in his bed, the sleeping Leah and baby beside him, he strained his ears. He heard the moan of the wind and the creak of the old house. He rose from the bed, slipped across to the window, drew back the thick curtain and peered out. All he could see was the sweep of snow as it scudded through the icy blackness. He must have imagined the dog's howl. He returned to the welcome warmth of his blankets. Maybe he'd been dreaming.

Come next morning, he pulled on his coat and boots. Snow was still falling, the wind having veered from south to north, and he had to struggle through a drift to make his way. He called the dog, but there was no response.

The door of the shed was partly open. He called the dog again. Suddenly there was a movement, and Jack blundered into the doorway. Something was wrong, yet the animal's tail gamely wagged from side to side to greet his master. Peering closely, Angus grunted with dismay. The dog's eyes showed a strange opaqueness that was tinged with the redness of blood. Jack had clearly been rubbing at his pain-filled sockets, and as he started forward he bumped into the shed's doorframe. He was blind. Angus gathered him up in his arms and struggled through the snow, back to the house.

Meanwhile, Leah had got the fire started, feeding it with wood, but at Angus's entry she straightened up.

'What's happened?'

He gently rested the dog down on the floor, close to the fire.

'Some devil's got at him,' he said. 'Seems to me, they've splashed something in his eyes, maybe acid.'

Leah cupped Jack's head in her hands, gazed at his eyes. 'Who would do such a thing?'

'The same person who killed our horses,' Angus said.

The dog lay trustingly as they bathed his eyes with warm water, but it was to no avail. Whatever had been splashed into his eyes had achieved its purpose. The dog would never be able to see again. The sheer spitefulness of the deed was sickening.

The baby came awake in her cradle, began to cry.

What would happen next in this terrible cycle of events? Apart from his own, were the lives of Leah and Anna now at risk? He didn't voice his thoughts. He knew the same fears haunted his wife, for she went to the baby, lifted her from the cradle and held her close.

Shortly afterwards, the Spencer held

55

ready, Angus ventured outside again, seeking sign of tracks around the shed and elsewhere, but the snow was falling so thickly that any sign had long been obscured. He cursed and shuddered, feeling as bleak as the weather.

During subsequent days Jack did not adapt well to a sightless life and frequently became disorientated. Angus considered shooting the dog, but Leah would not hear of it. 'He has been a loyal friend for so many years. Now he needs loyalty from us.'

On reflection, Angus agreed.

Meanwhile, he wondered whether it was safe for them to remain at the ferry house. Was the objective of his mysterious enemy to drive him away? He wondered why they had not struck at him directly. It would have been easy enough to shoot at him from the surrounding forest, or even gun him down as he rode the trail to and from town. It was almost as if his enemy was playing with him, a sort of cat-and-mouse game.

His mind swung again to Johnny Kypp. If Kypp was his persecutor he would have to strike back, but it would be difficult. There was no regularity in the attacks. It could be weeks or months before the next strike — or tomorrow. In between attacks Kypp could be out of the territory, miles away.

Angus was obliged to adopt a continual siege mentality, forever watching his back and guarding those who were precious to him. Life was becoming intolerable.

But when he broached the subject of moving away to Leah she looked up from her Bible and would not hear of it.

'You've done nothing wrong, Angus. We mustn't be driven away by evil men. God says we must work out our own salvation, for He works within us.'

She came to him and slipped her arms around his neck. 'And I agree with Him,' she whispered.

Presently, he knelt and prayed with his wife. Inwardly he promised himself that, if he had to, he would kill to protect his little family.

★ ★ ★

The last of the winter dragged away until the ice in the river melted, the snow crusted and thawed, and spring brought greenery and flowers to the land.

'It's like a dark grave has been opened up,' Leah exclaimed, 'opened up to let the Lord's blessing in.'

But the tension did not slacken in Angus. He retained a constant vigil, and the strain made him impatient and irritable, sometimes showing a sharpness to Leah and Ed Mullins that was not natural to him. Every time he looked at Jack the dog, seeing him struggle around in his blindness, he was reminded of the wicked forces that had smitten them. Angus had heard that dogs, when they lost their sight, had the ability to find their way by scent — but Jack was not one of these. Had he and

Leah not been alert, the poor animal would have fallen into the river more than once.

But the spring blossomed into summer; Leah had again planted her vegetable-and-herb patch; and there were no further 'events'.

'Maybe all those evil things,' Leah said hopefully, 'are in the past now.'

Angus smiled. 'Maybe your prayers have been answered.'

Slowly they began to believe that their normal lives could resume. They even enjoyed picnics in the meadow and Leah would read aloud from her Bible. Anna was developing sturdy limbs and her gurgling sounds were as near to talking as any babe could get and she loved the dolly that Leah had made for her.

But the past had not gone away.

One day, having left Ed Mullins to operate the ferry, Angus was in town and stepped into the saloon to slake his thirst. As he thrust his way through the doors, he almost collided with somebody and for a second Angus found himself gazing into the dark and brooding eyes that he would never forget — nor the pock-marked face and braided hair. Then the other man glanced away, moving quickly into the street.

He had encountered Johnny Kypp. Five years in prison had weathered him. His body had filled out; no doubt his muscles had been developed by the hard labour of work gangs, but there was no mistaking him. When Angus gazed after him, he had disappeared into a side-alley.

Angus didn't linger over his drink. He was soon on his way back home, praying that Kypp hadn't already perpetrated some wickedness. He also kept a steady watch on the surrounding terrain, wondering if the outlaw might be lurking somewhere, waiting to ambush him. But he arrived back safely, greatly relieved as he found that nothing untoward had happened during his absence.

He suspected that Kypp might strike this very night, and he decided to set a trap. Accordingly, come dusk, he left Ed Mullins in the ferry house to safeguard Leah and the baby. Then he set his two valuable horses in the meadow and took up position in a clump of trees close by. Crouching down in the shadow, he had his Spencer ready and remained wide awake, tensing at the crack of every twig or movement of wild creatures. But after long hours of vigilance, nothing of note had occurred, and dawn brought a blanket of silver dew and a pinkish glow in the eastern sky.

Angus returned his horses to the safety of the barn and Ed Mullins emerged from the house to prepare the animals for their work. The following night, they reversed positions, Ed taking his turn on watch, but again they suffered no intrusion. If Johnny Kypp was intent on further mischief, he was taking his time about it.

It was twenty-four hours later that events took a frightening turn.

6

As the moon became hazed over prior to giving way to the first paleness preceding dawn, Angus came to full wakefulness, his grip on his Spencer tightening. He felt his insides quiver. Ed Mullins had taken a well-deserved night off and was in town. Angus cursed himself for having dozed, but lack of sleep over recent nights was really getting to him and he knew that if things continued this way, his daytime alertness would also become dulled.

While night-time guards were maintained, he had allowed his replacement draught-horses the freedom of grazing. He crouched within his hog-pen, scarcely aware of the sleeping beasts in the shelter behind him. The pen was not the ideal place to spend the night, but it provided cover that was both concealing and protective, and from it he was afforded reasonable vision of his land and buildings.

It was easier to imagine movement than to see it. More than once he'd raised his rifle, tense and taut, suspecting some stealthy approach which turned out to be purely in his mind.

But now he felt certain he heard some small sound, maybe the snapping of an underfoot twig, from alongside the meadow. He strained his eyes into the gloom. He saw nothing untoward until he noticed how the horses had raised their heads and were showing nervousness.

Then he saw the briefest flurry of movement close in against his barn, and almost immediately the flicker of flame showed. He was on his feet immediately, the rifle into his shoulder. As if in response to his action, a target presented itself — the darting figure of an intruder, showing like a black spider against the lighter shade of the barn's wall. Angus's finger tightened on the trigger and the Spencer roared, punching a fiery blast through the gloom. Within a second, retaliation came. The hollow snap of a six-shooter cut through the rifle's reverberating detonation and lead thudded spitefully into the wooden pen-wall.

Angus had lost sight of the intruder, but he had seen the orange flame of six-shooter fire and he fired his repeater again, the boom of the gunfire having the horses in the meadow whinnying in fright. His target had disappeared but record of his presence remained as a golden plume erupted from the barn, painting the overhead clouds with a flickering reflection. With little rain of late the barn was tinder-dry and was soon fully ablaze. He was running towards the old building, when the thought struck him that this could easily be a diversion. His enemy might well now be between him and the house.

With his concern for Leah and Anna mounting, he twisted around, ran desperately up to the house, not caring that he was presenting an easy target. A lantern had flared in the upstairs room, and increased fear lifted panic into his throat.

He reached the porch, leaping up the steps, relieved that the main door was closed, but he knew that it would be easy for somebody to force their way in from the back of the house. He plunged inside, immediately aware of Anna's cries. And then, glancing up, he saw Leah peering down at him from the trap-door.

'What's happened, honey?' she gasped.

'Somebody's set fire to the barn,' he cried. 'I must get over there, see what I can do.'

He was turning back, relieved that Leah was safe, when he realized that she still might not be. Once he turned his back to attend to the fire, she would be as vulnerable as she had been before. He climbed halfway up on the ladder, passed the gun to her.

'Take it,' he instructed. 'If anybody comes near you, use it!'

'But, Angus, you'll be unarmed.'

'I'll use a pitchfork if I have to.'

He delayed no more, but hastened from the house, seeing that the barn was now a mass of billowing flame, roaring like a locomotive. The roof was crumbling in white-hot ash. He prayed that the intruder had left the area, having struck his blow, and, with daylight not far away, was no longer seeking trouble. Even so, he gazed around with great apprehension.

The name of Johnny Kypp kept hammering into his mind. He must go to the town marshal once more, attempt to goad him into finding and arresting this individual who, Angus was convinced, was making life an absolute misery.

As he set to work tackling the flames, Leah came out to help him, placing Anna, blanket-wrapped, in a sheltered spot. They hauled buckets of water up from the river, dousing everything they could, their eyes watering and stinging, their skin and clothing blackened by smoke. Fortunately there had been no livestock or anything else of great value inside. All along he'd considered the barn a place where his enemy, or enemies, might strike. So he had left it largely empty, but even so the structure had been part of his estate, part of his heritage, built by the hard labour of his father many years since, and to see flame licking through its old timbers was sickening.

By full daylight, they had done the best they could, although the place was ruined, blackened and charred, and would never be of practical purpose again.

When Ed Mullins arrived from town he was shocked at what he saw and at the story Angus related. But within a couple of hours it was business as usual as the first clients of the day trickled in and were ferried over the river, their eyebrows raised in surprise as they saw the wreck of the barn.

Angus rode Judas hard into town, determined that the law must respond to what was happening, give him some protection. He found Marshal Fred Terrill in his office, chewing on a dead, half-smoked cigar as he thumbed through some paperwork. Terrill was of cumbersome build; he had a reputation for laziness and overindulgence of the bottle, being a far different man from his conscientious predecessor, Jim Ringrose. He waved his visitor towards a chair, but Angus was in no mood for relaxation.

In a breathless voice he related the details of the latest outrage.

Terrill shook his head despairingly, stubbed out his cigar. 'I helped you in guardin' your place,' he said, 'but you probably know you're outside my jurisdiction out there. The state's lines of responsibility have been shifted. This is rightly a job for the county sheriff. I heard he's a sick man at present.'

Angus grunted with frustration.

'This fellow Johnny Kypp,' he said, 'do you know anything about him?'

'Not much,' Terrill shrugged, 'apart

from the fact that he got sentenced for robbin' the bank, five or six years back, but you know all about that. He's done his time. I got nothin' against him now.'

'Well, he's out of jail and I saw him in town the other day. Seems too coincidental that my barn got burned.'

Terrill scratched his stubbly jaw reflectively. 'Come to think about it, the Kypp family run a smallholdin' over at Eagle Springs, but I think you're makin' a mountain from a molehill. Kypp's most likely got nothin' to do with your troubles. Still, to put your mind at rest, you might care to take a ride over there and see what the Kypps have to say. They won't make you welcome, though.'

'Eagle Springs.' Angus nodded. 'That's south of Kelly's Hole.' He rammed his hat on. 'Thanks for your help.' And he left Terrill to his paperwork and wished that old Marshal Ringrose still ruled the roost.

He was reluctant to spend any more time away from the ferry house than was necessary because he knew that Mullins could not protect Leah and Anna every second of the day; he was too busy ferrying travellers across the river. But Angus was determined to confront Johnny Kypp and have things out with him.

His was relieved, on arrival at home, to find that no trouble had occurred during his absence, except that Jack the old collie had been afflicted by a fit. Leah sat nursing the blind animal, even laying her hands on his head and praying for a cure. But come next morning he was dead — and it seemed just one more blow in the succession of tragedies that had befallen them, another misfortune caused by their enemies.

After Angus had buried Jack in the meadow they both felt pretty low. He discussed matters with Leah, expressing his conviction that he must visit the Kypp homestead and try to glean some idea of what was going on.

'You must be careful, honey,' Leah

warned, her arm around Anna. 'Don't incite any violence.'

'I'll try to sort things out without stirring up more trouble, but this situation is getting crazy. We can't go on like this.'

Leah nodded sombrely, knowing that he was right, wishing that God would be a little quicker in answering her prayers.

Next afternoon, Angus told Ed Mullins what he was doing, saddled Judas, kissed his wife and child and rode out. He knew that the undertaking was risky in more ways than one, but anger simmered inside of him. He would not court violence, but if he was offered no alternative, he would not flinch away from it. The Spencer rifle was nestled in his saddle scabbard and he had recently invested in a long-barrelled Navy Colt which was holstered at his hip. His practising with it had brought a frown to Leah's face but she had not commented, realizing that this world had many aspects that were not of her choosing.

On the way to Eagle Springs Angus stopped overnight at a guest-house in the small township of Kelly's Hole. The lady proprietor, a tough old bird, gave him directions to the Kypp small-holding.

'But you be careful,' she said. 'Old Linus Kypp is as mean as a skunk. He don't take to strangers, and he treats his wife Arabella like trash.'

'How about his son Johnny?' Angus enquired, trying to show a casualness he did not feel.

'Ain't seen him more than once or twice since he came out o' jail,' the woman responded, 'but I guess he's tarred with the same brush as his pa.'

Angus nodded his thanks.

Next morning he started out at daybreak. He knew that there was no guarantee that Johnny would be at home. Even at this moment he might be hovering close to the ferry house, intent on further mischief. Angus hoped not to delay his absence any longer than was absolutely necessary.

For a couple of hours he followed the trail through heavily timbered country where the trees were redolent with spring's blossom and chipmunks frolicked in the branches. He wondered how the land could appear so beautiful while black hatred inhabited men's hearts, even his own.

Mid-morning, with the sun burning from the cloudless sky like an angry eye, he reached the southern end of the valley of Eagle Springs and he soon located the Kypp homestead. He reined in Judas on a ridge overlooking the run-down establishment; it was crouched like a dark bird waiting to flap its wings and rise into the wind. It consisted of a rusty corrugated iron shack, with a big oak tree at its front, a barn and some outlying chicken and hog-pens.

He gazed at the abode, seeing no sign of life, though the door stood open. He knew better than to sashay in without giving warning. Johnny Kypp might be at home, watching out through the window and there was no sense in stirring him into violence unnecessarily, though the thought that he might be close to the man who had made his life such a misery had fury running through his veins.

He lifted his hands into a cup about his mouth and called out: 'Hello there! I'd like to come visiting!'

He waited. There was no response apart from the crowing of a cockerel from the yard. Otherwise the throbbing silence remained unbroken. He debated whether to call out again, but decided against it. Instead, he slipped his Spencer from its scabbard, pulled back the hammer and heeled Judas forward down the slope. As he got nearer the cabin, he knew that he was a sitting target, but impatience to sort matters out drove him on.

When he was a few yards from the open doorway, he reined-in his horse and called again: 'Hello there!'

It was then the girl appeared in the

doorway. She looked Mexican and had long, black hair. He guessed her age was no more than twenty. She wore a multi-coloured bead necklace and a calico dress of pale blue that hugged her hips and thighs, and accentuated her breasts. There was a wantonness about her that he found disturbing.

Angus took a deep, steadying breath. 'I'm looking for Johnny Kypp,' he said.

She shook her head. 'Johnny? He not here.'

'And Linus?'

'My husband,' she said, 'he not in the house.'

Her words disappointed him.

He wondered how on earth had old man Linus got himself such a young wife. One thing was sure: she couldn't be Johnny's mother because he was older than her, and there was more Indian about him than Mexican.

But now he realized that her gaze extended beyond him; she was looking over his shoulder. He felt the small hairs along his spine tingling.

The voice came strongly.

'Stay where you are, mister, or you're dead! Drop that gun and raise your hands.'

Angus, still in the saddle, cursed. He'd been out-foxed. He dropped his Spencer, not to the ground but into its saddle-scabbard. Then he grudgingly lifted his hands.

7

He heard the rustling noise of somebody descending from the oak tree
behind him. The man now threatening
him must have been perched up on a
branch, watching every move he made.
When Angus risked a glance over his
shoulder, he saw a wizened, grey-haired
individual in a black hat moving with
surprising agility, keeping his rifle, a
huge .50 calibre Sharps buffalo gun,
deadly steady. At such close range,
Angus knew that the slightest pressure
on the trigger would blast his head from
his shoulders.

The old man circled around, and
stepped up on to the porch alongside
the girl. Angus had never seen such an
ill-matched couple. Linus must have
been well over sixty. His face was
weather-beaten, carrying scars that
could have been made with a knife

blade. Where he had sweated in the heat, salt had encrusted on the deep-etched scar-lines. The black stubs of his teeth showed between lips that were no more than twin flakes of dried-out skin. He was bandy and dwarf-like and had the same brooding eyes as those of Johnny Kypp. Those eyes held a glint of insanity. There was no doubt he was Johnny's father. His squat figure reminded Angus of a distorted image in a fairground mirror.

'Do not do wicked things, Linus,' Arabella warned. 'He far too pretty to bloody up.'

'God a'mighty, keep your hungry eyes away from him!' Linus snarled, but his attention remained riveted on Angus. 'Now, Troon, I know who you are and what you did, gettin' Johnny locked away like that, blackening my good name. So it's no good makin' out you're somebody else. You got no right to come here. You ain't welcome.'

'Mr Kypp,' Angus said, keeping his voice levelled, 'I want to speak to Johnny.'

The old man scowled. 'Johnny ain't here.' A gobbet of spit accompanied his words. 'He don't live here no more. But wherever he is, he's served his time and he don't want the likes of you sniffin' after him. You just leave him alone.'

Angus had come a long way. He didn't favour being fobbed off so easily. 'I got reason to believe that Johnny has killed two of my horses and burned my barn down.'

Linus Kypp unleashed a growl, his hands white knuckled on the Sharps. 'You can't prove nothin', but I'll warn you, if you come pesterin' me or my son, it'll be the last thing you ever do!'

Suddenly Arabella Kypp spoke up from behind her husband, her voice shrill. 'Best you leave, Señor Troon. Linus — he means what he say!'

'All right, have your way,' Angus said. 'But things won't end here.'

He lowered his hands, touched his heels to Judas's flanks and turned away. He rode off at a trot, not looking over his shoulder, but he could feel Kypp's eyes burning into him and he feared that at any moment the man might blast off his gun, shooting him in the back. Gradually he left the homestead behind and he breathed more easily. He was annoyed with himself. He had gleaned nothing in coming here, except maybe the realization that old Linus Kypp was as stirred up against him as was his son Johnny.

He reached the far side of the valley, reined in and took a glance towards the homestead, but the great oak tree hampered his view and he couldn't see whether either husband or wife were still on their porch. He edged Judas into the pines that clothed the valleyside and started to climb, appreciating that at least he was out of rifle range. He wondered where Johnny Kypp was. He was concerned that he might, at this very moment, be hovering in the vicinity of the ferry house, intent on committing evil.

On the other hand, Johnny Kypp might be no more than a stone's throw from his father's homestead — or even hiding out within it. But Angus dismissed the latter idea, believing that Johnny wasn't the hiding sort. Had he been there, he would have no doubt welcomed Angus with a bullet.

When he had reached the high rim of the valley he again made a halt and gazed back, his eyes meandering over the terrain. Everywhere, all nature, seemed to be holding its breath. He knew he was hidden up here in the trees, but his own view of the abode was no longer obscured. He waited for five minutes, cogitating on his next course of action, and all the time thoughts of Leah, Anna and Ed Mullins lingered his mind. He could hardly believe that Anna was now a year and a half old, the months had passed so quickly.

Even though Mullins coped with operating the ferry, he was by no means able. His spirit was as willing as ever, but age was beginning to take its toll, and poor eyesight and the stiffness of rheumatism troubled him. If some sudden danger struck, Ed's determination might not be enough to provide protection.

But, having journeyed to the Kypp place, Angus felt reluctant to call a halt to his investigations. He was convinced that the old man was hiding something. He decided to stay here on the slope, to keep watch on the place throughout the remaining daylight. The sun lazed over the distant hills, appearing to cover them with a pink organdie.

He dismounted, slaked his thirst from his canteen, then filled his hat with water and allowed Judas the same pleasure. He slackened off the sorrel's girth and hunkered down to watch. Throughout the long hours of the afternoon, everything remained as quiet as a locked-up graveyard. He could understand Leah's love of the wild places as opposed to the bustle of town life.

Eventually, with the sun sinking in its final glory over the western mountain rim, a coolness came to the air. Angus was aware of the tiredness in his bones. He'd had a long and tense day, and ahead of him lay a tedious ride back to the ferry house and the welcome of home.

But all at once his reverie was disturbed. He came to his feet impulsively as he saw movement on the far side of the valley — movement that gradually changed from an obscure, dark shape into the more clearly defined outline of a lone rider and horse moving steadily through the gloaming towards the homestead. Even at the distance Angus recognized the horse as a Morgan. The last time he'd seen the animal was as Johnny Kypp led it on to the ferry five years ago. The appearance of the fine horse had been stamped in his memory ever since. He slipped his Spencer from its scabbard.

Johnny Kypp was coming home, little suspecting that the victim of his callous torment might soon have him within the sights of his gun. Angus sensed that the awesome time of reckoning was at hand. He had never taken a life before, but this might be his chance to put an end to the gruesome events that had turned his world into a nightmare.

He decided to allow Kypp to reach the habitation. Once he was inside, he would approach on foot, taking advantage of any concealment. He would fire through the window if necessary. It was a sneaky way of killing, but he had been an undeserving victim for too long.

Gritting his teeth, his Spencer ready, he was about to move down the slope when events took a totally unexpected turn.

The heavy blast of a large-calibre gun boomed out from the doorway of the cabin, and with it the orange flash of the detonation. Angus watched as the approaching horseman was stopped in his tracks, the Morgan rearing in panic at the proximity of the bullet, its whinny piercing the echo of the thunderous gunfire. As if to reinforce the message of the first shot, a second blast roared. The rider fell from his rearing mount and lay unmoving on the ground as the animal galloped back the way it had come.

Angus was amazed. Had Linus Kypp done the job of gunning down Johnny on his behalf? But why . . . why should the old man have shot his son? Or could it have been Arabella who had fired the shots? But that possibility seemed no more plausible.

Once again a surprise lay in store. Through the gloom of the increasing dusk Angus saw movement stir within the fallen body, saw the man first prop himself groggily on to his arms, then slowly hoist himself on to his legs. Angus strained his eyes, striving desperately to establish that it was Johnny Kypp down there. Perhaps he'd been wrong in assuming the identity of the man. But, at that distance, try as he might he could see no distinguishing features, nothing to prove who he was or who he was not. Angus could only watch as the dim figure limped away through the fading light, clearly anxious to put as much space as he could between himself and the gun before a third shot felled him for good. Within a minute he had scurried into the fringe of dark trees that bordered the valley. Angus knew that, with darkness descending, he would never track the man down, nor would he solve the mystery as to why he had been repelled with such ferocity from reaching the habitation.

Angus returned to Judas, tightened the girth and swung into the saddle. There were a lot of unanswered questions, but now was not the time to resolve them. He set out on the long journey home, anxious to assure himself that all was well back there.

He would have been horrified had he known that he would find no such assurance.

8

Ed Mullins was slumped on the ground, blood seeping from his shoulder staining his shirt crimson; the shock of the bullet's impact was now giving way to intense, breath-cutting pain. He groaned, then coughed up some more blood.

Only a couple of hours ago, he'd waved farewell to Angus as the latter had set out for the distant Kypp homestead. In his handicapped voice, Ed had wished his employer well, promising him that he would keep an eye on things at the ferry. During the time that followed he'd had not a single traveller to ferry across the river, and had occupied himself with maintenance of the great cog-wheels housing the ropes that drew the barge back and forth, carefully oiling the mechanism.

While he was thus occupied the

bullet caught him, slamming into his shoulder, throwing him face forward, down the steep slope of the river bank. Stunned, he had sprawled there for a full minute, feeling the pain intensify, aware that blood was pumping from the wound. He had been unaware that any gunman had been in the vicinity, that any danger was threatening him.

But now, he heard a sound — a woman's frightened voice calling his name. 'Ed . . . Ed, what's happened!'

Leah had heard the shot and come running from the house, desperately searching for him. Even in his dazed state, Ed was conscious of the fear that the gunman might still be lurking — and that Leah could be his next target. Red mists were clouding his brain, but somehow he managed to shout out, 'Leah, stay back!'

Leah, holding her skirts high as she ran, heard the desperate cry, hesitated. She glanced around but saw nothing untoward. Everywhere seemed quiet. She stumbled in the direction from which Ed's voice had come. Drawing up breathlessly on the brink of the river bank, she glanced down and cried out in alarm. He was lying so still, his shirt a sodden gory mess. If he'd rolled another yard, he would have fallen into the water. She practically fell down the grassy bank, dropping to her knees beside Mullins, praying that he was not dead. It seemed God answered her pleading, for she could see Ed's chest rising and falling. But she had no doubt that unless she could stem the flow of blood from the ragged wound in his shoulder he would soon succumb.

With desperate hands she ripped a large piece from her petticoat, and made it into a pad. Then she tore another section to form a bandage which she bound over his shoulder and beneath his armpit. Her hands were slippery with his blood, but she worked undeterred. Only when she was convinced that she had stemmed the loss of blood, albeit temporarily, did she leave him and scramble up the bank to its top.

Who had fired that cowardly shot!

She gazed around, her hand shading her eyes against the sun. Everything looked so normal, so peaceful — yet she knew that what had happened was another example of the mindless succession of wicked deeds which had been carried out against her husband and those who were part of his life. And the fact that this enemy remained out of sight was no guarantee that he was not, even at this moment, spying on her from some hiding place, maybe laughing at her predicament, maybe already lining up his gun for another shot.

She flinched at the thought, but stood her ground, all the time praying to God for His help. She wished Angus were here, but he was miles away, tracking down the enemy they feared but who was, however, far nearer than they had imagined.

She strove to restore her calm. She would help nobody by remaining in a state of panic. Her thoughts swung to

Anna, whom she had left playing in the kitchen of the house; yet at this moment she must take the terrible risk of leaving the child unprotected.

She returned down the bank to Mullins. To her relief, he was regaining consciousness and groaning with the pain which tortured him. He was trying to scramble to his feet, and she supported him, finding strength she had not known she possessed.

'What happened, Ed?' she gasped. 'Did you see who shot you?'

His tongue struggled with his cleft palate to form words. She had to lean close to hear his faltering whisper. 'No. F-first thing I knew . . . I had a bullet in me. I . . . ' His speech trailed off, his pain too intense for discourse.

Somehow she got him across the meadow to the house and into the living-room. He virtually collapsed on to the sofa, and she struggled to prevent him from rolling on to the floor. She checked Anna, thankful that she appeared unharmed. Her attention returned to the wounded man.

Without Angus here she knew that the ferry would have to be closed for the rest of the day. One other thing was obvious. Unless Ed got medical attention promptly he would die. Maybe even with a doctor's attention, the bullet had gone too deep and would prove fatal. She debated rapidly what her next course of action should be. She could wait until a traveller turned up at the ferry and seek their help. But with things so desperately quiet today, it might be hours before somebody appeared, and, even then, they might not be prepared to assist. Anyway, by then Ed might have passed away. Alternatively, she could somehow get the patient into the buckboard wagon and take him to the doctor in town. She decided to adopt the latter option. She had no choice but to take Anna with her.

It took her ten minutes to harness the pony to the wagon, which had a canvas covering, and another ten to help

Mullins from the couch, across the porch and somehow get him into the wagon. She fetched a blanket and pillow for him. He seemed to be losing consciousness again.

'Don't die, Ed,' she whispered desperately. 'For God's sake don't die!' She knew she had no time to delay.

She re-entered the house, lifted Anna in her arms and carried her to the wagon, murmuring to her to be a good girl. She was pleased that the canvas provided shade for both her passengers. She climbed on to the wagon-seat, jerked on the reins and set the pony in motion, hoping that the bumpy trail would not bring further pain to Mullins.

She did not look back, did not see the man step from the concealment of the adjacent cottonwood. He stood for a moment, his lips widened into a wolfish grin. He gazed towards the rapidly departing wagon, and knew he was hidden by the cloud of dust trailing behind it.

Then he stepped towards the house. He fancied that woman. He'd watched her before, and the sight of her supple body and prissy ways had sent a tingle through his loins. Maybe he would have her before the day was out. He grunted as he considered the prospect. He'd wait until she got back.

* * *

Leah wished that her father was still alive, but God had claimed him just a year ago. How desperately she could do with his support at this time — but a new minister had now taken up the living. She stopped several times during the journey to town, checking to ensure that Mullins was still breathing and to attempt to quiet Anna who cried continuously, not liking the bump of the wagon on the rutted trail.

Leah could have stopped at the homes of friends, some Russian immigrants, whose smallholdings stood alongside the trail, but she was sure that time was vitally important. If only the medical powers she herself had been blessed with could have been strong enough, but she knew that it needed more than prayer and faith to extract a bullet. Only a skilled medical man could save this man who had served Angus so well.

On the outskirts of town she halted once more to check Ed's condition. She gasped with apprehension. She felt the pulse in his neck. He was still alive — but only just. She climbed aboard the wagon again and urged the tiring pony into motion. She entered the town, seeing how things were pretty quiet in the early afternoon heat. She made it up Main Street to the surgery of Doctor Clayton, drew rein and threw herself from the wagon seat, turning her ankle over in her haste.

She groaned with dismay as she saw that the doctor's surgery appeared to be closed and silent. Perhaps he was away, called out for some other emergency. She thumped on his door, bruising her hands. She waited, her lips moving as she murmured over and over: 'Please God may he be here!'

At last she heard a sound from within and the door swung open. Jasmine Clayton, the doctor's wife appeared, her hands covered in flour.

'Is he here,' Leah gasped. 'The doctor . . . '

Jasmine Clayton needed no further hastening, seeing the desperation in Leah's eyes. She nodded, turned back and called to her husband. 'Edmund, come quick!'

Within seconds Edmund Clayton appeared, drying his hands on a towel. He was tall, and this was emphasized by his thinness and hollow cheeks. But he had a reputation as a fine doctor.

'Ed Mullins,' Leah cried, nodding towards the wagon. 'He's been shot!'

The doctor moved quickly, hauling himself up beneath the canopy. Both Leah and Jasmine Clayton followed him, but there was no room for them all in the wagon. Leah lifted the wide-eyed

Anna out and held her. They stood back, watching the doctor kneeling beside Mullins. Leah was filled with dread. Perhaps she was already too late. It seemed an eternity that the medical man took over his examination. He pressed his ear to his patient's chest, after which he checked the pulse. At last he straightened up.

'Will he live?' Leah asked anxiously.

The doctor shook his head, his face gaunt. 'I'm afraid he's dead,' he said.

⋆ ⋆ ⋆

Giddiness assailed Leah like a green mist. Jasmine Clayton took hold of Anna. Leah felt unable to breathe and Elizabeth, the doctor's seventeen-year-old daughter reached out to support her.

'Dead,' Leah murmured 'He can't be . . .'

But Edmund Clayton was solemnly nodding. 'Best go inside. I'll see to things outside.'

The two women helped Leah into the house, sat her down. The place was redolent with the smell of lemon polish. Leah slumped with her head in her hands, unable to accept the cruel turn of events. Jasmine fetched a drink while her daughter sat alongside Leah, striving to find comforting words.

Meanwhile Doctor Clayton had Ed Mullin's body transferred to the town's mortuary and arranged for a man to attend to the pony and wagon. Clayton crossed the street to the marshal's office. He had to inform the lawman that murder had been committed. It had occurred on land not under Marshal Terrill's jurisdiction, but it would be his duty to notify the county sheriff. Not that he felt he could rely on Fred Terrill. He was in a constant drunken haze and rumour had it that he was running up huge gambling debts.

The doctor's fears were proved valid. Upon entering the lawman's office, he was assailed by the stench of liquor; the marshal was leaning back in his chair, his eyes vacant, an empty bottle on the desk before him. He scarcely nodded as Clayton related events, but he seemed to understand the instruction to telegraph the county sheriff, though whether he would remember to do it was another matter. Clayton would check later.

He wasted no further time with Terrill but returned to his home where his wife was holding smelling salts beneath Leah's nostrils. Poor Leah had received a terrible shock, but she was now regaining her composure, sitting up and drying her tears.

'Who did it?' Clayton enquired.

Leah shook her head. 'I was in the house when I heard the shot. By the time I got outside, there was no sign of anybody. I found Ed by the river. He'd fallen down the bank. I thought . . . I thought I could get him here in time to save his life.'

'There was nothing more you could have done,' Jasmine Clayton murmured soothingly.

'Where's Angus?' the doctor asked.

Leah explained events as best she could. When she'd finished, Clayton said that he'd heard they'd had trouble at the ferry, about the burning of the barn, but he hadn't realized that matters had got so bad.

Leah spent several hours with the Claytons, gradually coming to terms with the awful events of the day. Eventually she decided it was time to get back to the ferry house. Angus would be returning soon and she needed to be there to let him know what had happened. Doctor Clayton insisted that he accompanied her, and although she claimed she would be all right, that whoever had done the shooting would be long gone, he insisted.

Accordingly, they left town as it was getting dark, the grey sky already tinged with a sullen blue-black over the east. The doctor drove the wagon, Leah and the child under the canvas, with Clayton's horse fastened to a tie-ring at the back. It was dark by the time they reached the vicinity of the ferry and Leah was greatly relieved to see a light showing from the window.

'Angus is home,' she said. 'Thank God for that!' But she dreaded having to impart the awful news to him.

'I'll be all right now,' she said. 'You can go back. Doctor Clayton, I am so grateful for all you have done for me.'

The doctor had halted the wagon. He debated whether to see her safely inside the house, but he knew that he had taken a risk in being away from his surgery, so, finding comfort from the distant glow of the light, he stepped down and unhitched his horse.

Leah repeated her thanks. 'I know Angus will be in touch with you.'

He nodded, clasping her hand in his own thin fingers for a moment, then he turned to his horse, mounted up and rode off.

Leah climbed on to the wagon seat, flicked the reins and set the pony towards the house, little realizing the awesome fate that awaited her.

9

She drove the wagon into the barn and loosened the harness, thinking that she would return to unhitch the pony once she had informed Angus of events. She gathered up the sleeping Anna, walked to the house, and stepped up on to the porch. The door stood partly open, the light glowing from within.

'Angus!' she called, stepping inside.

The main room stood empty, but she heard movement from the kitchen.

'Angus!' she repeated. She heard footsteps and suddenly her heart missed a beat. In the doorway stood a man she had never seen before. She felt the blood draining from her face and her frightened mind registered how foolish she had been to send the doctor home and come on alone.

'Where's Angus?' she somehow got out.

The stranger smiled licentiously. 'Ain't no need to tremble like a leaf, ma'am. Angus ain't here, so you don't have to worry none about him.'

'Where is he?' she repeated.

His stubbly face was creased in a grin. 'Can't say I rightly know where the dear man is, 'ceptin' he ain't where he should be, looking after his sweet little wife.'

She was making a brave attempt to steady herself, but his eyes were burning into her, somehow, she imagined, seeing through her clothing to her naked body.

'Who are you?' she got out.

'I'm an old . . . acquaintance of your husband, Mrs Troon, or may I call you Leah. I'm sure your Angus won't mind you showing me a little hospitality.'

He took a pace forward.

'Why are you here?' she gasped, trying to stem his advance with her question.

He rubbed his shoulder. 'Thing is, I've got this stiffness in my shoulder. It kinda catches when I move. I heard word in town that you could fix this sort of thing, that you had some sort of heavenly gift that could cure folks' aches and pains. That's so, ain't it?'

Leah realized she was utterly at his mercy. Holding Anna, she knew he would catch her in a flash if she attempted to escape him. She reckoned her best hope was to try and humour this man, and pray, *please God*, that Angus would return before she came to any harm. She was still unable to stem the tremble that was in her, but she tried desperately not to show fear.

'It's true,' she said, 'I can help with some afflictions, but I must prepare my oils. It'll take time.'

She forced herself to walk slowly forward. She placed Anna down. The child sat wide-eyed on the floor, unable to understand what was happening, but sharing her mother's fear none the less.

'There's no need for oils,' he said, 'Just a little warmth from your hands will do the trick, I'm sure.'

'But . . .'

'No oils, Leah Troon,' he insisted, the grin on his face replaced by a glint of impatience.

'I'll just use this,' she gasped, reaching out to grasp the cup of pepper she had kept in case she needed to defend herself one day. It had always been a joke between her and Angus, but now she prayed that if she was to hurl it into his eyes he might be deterred.

'Sit down,' she instructed, moving a chair out from the table for him. 'Which shoulder is it?'

He stepped towards her and fear slammed through her. 'Maybe we'll attend to that after.'

'After what?' she asked, then hurled the pepper into his face.

It had little effect apart from increasing his anger. She fought him then, fought him with every ounce of strength in her body, biting, kicking, clawing, screaming. For a second she broke free of him, turning away, but his strong hands clamped around her waist, twisted her back, his grip like steel. In a wild stumble, they both tripped and fell, his weight on top, pinning her down.

His crazed face was forced into hers. His evil breath, smelling of onions and whiskey, was suffocating her. She clenched her teeth; in vain she tried to turn away. He was too strong, too heavy, forcing his repulsive lips against hers, his tongue into her mouth, pushing her neck back so hard she thought it would break. She gasped, choking and gagging. She bit his tongue with all her might, tasting his blood.

Then he went mad.

★　★　★

It was well into the small hours when Angus set the weary Judas across the meadow fronting the ferry house. He was surprised to see, despite the lateness of the hour, that a light was showing from with in. He wondered whether Anna was unwell, whether

Leah was up tending to her. He was pleased that he had arranged with Ed Mullins to stay overnight and look after things.

He went directly to the stable to unsaddle his sorrel and was surprised to find the pony still hitched to the wagon. Uncharacteristically, Leah and Mullins must have forgotten him — but why would they have used the wagon anyway? He quickly unharnessed the pony and forked his rack high with hay. Then, after doing the same for Judas, he stepped towards the house.

The door stood open, displaying the lighted room within. He saw the inside furnishings in disarray — a chair on its side, smashed dishes on the floor. With a quickening heartbeat, he leapt up onto the porch, calling out: 'Leah!'

There was no response.

His nostrils were assailed by the smell of pepper.

Sure enough, the room looked as if it had been the scene of a struggle. He called her name desperately, going to the foot of the ladder which led to the loft bedroom. Leah would never have slept through his shouting, nor the baby — yet no answer came, no welcoming call, and panic took hold of him. Ed Mullins should have been bedded down upon the sofa, but there was no sign of him.

And then Angus heard the groan and, drawn by the sound, he pulled aside the sofa and found Leah lying on the floor. Leah, nigh naked, with her dress ripped away, blood and bruising darkening her pale skin, and unmistakable bite marks etched into her neck.

Oh God!

Angus sank to his knees, crying out with rage. He gathered her in his arms, lifted her against him, fearing that she was dead, but suddenly aware of her heart beating and the warmth that her body exuded. His lips pleaded with her, begging her to realize that she was safe now, that the nightmare was over.

'Leah, Leah . . . my sweet Leah!'

And as if in answer to his pleading,

her eyelids flickered up and he found himself gazing into blue eyes that were so familiar to him yet now showed nothing but terror.

'No!' she screamed, so loudly that it made him shudder.

Shocked, he pleaded with her. 'Leah, I'm here. It's Angus. You're safe, my love!'

Her expression hardened into a look of pure hatred. 'Go away . . . go away . . . go away!' and then she screamed with high-pitched desperation, the sound burning his ears.

She struggled as he raised her up, carried her around the sofa and rested her gently down. He attempted to soothe her with words that seemed useless. Only when she was totally exhausted, totally drained from her screaming did she go quiet — quiet until she spoke words that haunted him for the rest of his life.

'Anna's gone! He's taken Anna!'

'Who . . . who's taken her?' he stammered.

For a moment she breathed heavily, her brow furrowed with the intensity of thought, then she gave her head a despairing shake.

He answered for her. 'It was Kypp,' he got out, 'Johnny Kypp?' He was trembling with emotion, with hatred.

Her head dropped back. She had no strength. She writhed for a moment, a deep cry of distress in her throat, then her eyes closed. He watched, stunned, wretched with horror.

Johnny Kypp. The name tortured his brain like a white-hot branding-iron.

He hugged the limp body of his wife against him and sobbed. His heart felt crushed within his chest. Questions pounded at him. Why hadn't he quit this place at the first sign of trouble? Why had he left Leah so unprotected? Where was Ed Mullins? And where was his sweet little lass, Anna?

He gritted his teeth with anger. Somebody would have to pay for what had happened.

★　★　★

Angus Troon sat out the remainder of the night with Leah cradled in his arms. She was restless and tortured, throwing her eyes around, totally incoherent with her rambling. Come dawn, he washed her as best he could, cursing as he saw how her body had been abused. Finally, he wrapped her in a blanket and carried her to the stable. He rested her down in the bed of the wagon, noting how the floorboards were bloodstained. Why? And where was Mullins?

He harnessed the pony and within five minutes he was heading for town, not realizing that less than twenty-four hours earlier, Leah had made the same journey.

He glanced back at her. She was lying perfectly still, but he saw the movement of her eyes.

Little Anna was constantly on his mind. He remembered Sunday morning when he'd painted a funny face on an egg, and how she had smiled. His cheeks were moist with tears.

What had they done to her? Had their cruel hands smothered her to death? Or beaten her? Or discarded her small body to the ravages of the wild? He shuddered. Maybe he should have gone searching for her, trying to strike up a trail, but he knew that he had to get Leah to the doctor. She had been both physically and mentally tortured to distraction.

10

What followed was a nightmare for Angus. The Clayton family did everything they could to ease his pain. The thin doctor naturally told him of the events preceding the discovery of Leah in her distressed state; he bitterly reproached himself for not accompanying her into the house the previous night. And Angus's misery was increased as he learned about Ed Mullins's death.

The Claytons offered Angus and Leah accommodation during this traumatic period. The truth was that Leah could not be left alone and needed frequent sedation. In addition to the doctor's care, Jasmine and young Elizabeth were kindness personified.

But Angus did not have much time to show his appreciation. He prevailed upon Town Marshal Terrill, for once in a sober state, to assist him on the very next day in his efforts to track down his enemy — and, more important, Anna. But he was alarmingly aware that a man as uncouth, callous and merciless as the rapist and killer would have little patience with a young child and would soon grow tired of her, whatever his motives.

Angus and the marshal rode out to the now deserted ferry house, examining the stable and surrounding ground for any evidence — any horse-tracks, footprints or empty shell-cases. He went to the house, pausing on the threshold, needing to accustom himself to its stillness, its smell, its absences. In a state of numbness, he searched inside for any clue, but apart from the general disorder in the living-room and a larder that had been denuded, he found nothing of use.

He was convinced that whoever had committed the crime would have been unable to cross the river. He and Terrill scrutinized the trees and hills north of the ferry house, periodically meeting up to see if either had discovered anything. And at each meeting Angus could see the marshal's interest flagging. No doubt he was more concerned about his next drink in the saloon than tracing a lost child. Eventually Angus dismissed him, saying he wished to search further afield. Terrill departed without hesitation.

Angus continued his efforts into the late afternoon, his eyes combing the ground along the river bank and further afield, but in him was the sinking feeling that the man he sought and Anna were long gone. Come nightfall, he lingered at the house to make a sign, nailing it to a post which he drove into the ground: *Regret Ferry Service Suspended until Further Notice — Due to Illness.*

He made everything as secure as he could, though little seemed to matter any more. He opened up the hog-pen and chicken-run, released Leah's beloved goat Mary, letting the creatures out to forage for themselves in the wild. Then, he roped the draught-horses and the pony together, riding Judas himself, and, with a heavy heart, he led the small cavalcade back to Pawnee Bend. On arrival, he left his animals at the livery, ensuring they were given a double bait of oats.

Over the next days he rode to adjacent settlements and ranches, asking if there had been any sightings of Johnny Kypp or of the child — but everywhere his questions were met with blank expressions and shaking heads. It seemed that man and child had disappeared from the face of the earth. He had handbills run off at the printer's in town, appealing for information, and pinned them up everywhere he went.

On the fourth day he rode into high country beyond the Peigan. This was wild, lonely territory, not for the timid. Climbing through forests of fir, spruce and aspen, he reached the edge of a high precipitous cliff. Above, he spotted a bald eagle drifting on the thermals.

116

Leaving Judas tethered well back, he went down on his hands and knees, crawling to the very edge. He shuddered. He was no coward, but dizzy heights had always scared him. Now, he gazed into the grey, rocky vastness, hoping that he might sight something, anything, that would help him in his search, but all that caught his eye was the swirl of birds about their cliff-face nests and a whitewater stream far beneath, surging through the canyon like a tormented serpent.

As he withdrew from the crest he noticed something glinting in the grass. He discovered an empty bean-can. And then he saw something else. Back in the trees a large slab of rock provided a sort of natural lean-to, the rudest hooden. Sticks, long rotted, had been heaped as walls at the side to keep out the wind. The whole place merged almost indistinguishably into its mottled background. Within it the earth had been blackened by fire. Somebody had camped here, but not recently. Could it be the enemy he hunted?

He searched around and presently found an ingeniously made wooden crate. Its sides bore skilfully carved designs of wolves, coyotes and spiders. Ritual and dream figures with the power of *poha* of Indian mythology. He realized that this was a contraption used by the Osage tribe, so called 'people of the middle waters', to store the game they had killed until they returned for it. It was like a meat-safe. They would dangle it over the edge of the cliff on a rope, and thus prevent wild bear or any other creature from stealing it. But it had clearly been many years since this particular box had been used.

Angus examined it, seeing how it would be just large enough to take a human body. Beyond that, it divulged nothing in any way useful to him. It was just a relic of bygone days. This campsite itself had probably been used by Indians, and he had no quarrel with them, though the sooner they were all shipped off to the Indian Territories the safer the country would be.

* * *

On the fifth day, back at Pawnee Bends, he went to Ed Mullins's funeral. The poor man had always been a loner with no family and, apart from himself and the kind-hearted Claytons, the attendance was minimal. Leah was far too ill to attend; Elizabeth remained at home to look after her.

After that Leah's condition seemed to deteriorate; the blankness remained in her once lively eyes, which showed not a glimpse of recognition when Angus returned from his fruitless searches. She no longer spoke or communicated or went outside; she sat all the time in the same chair, her blonde head slumped, her face chalk-white. She had to be supported to the outhouse and washed. She had no appetite for food and had to be coaxed by hand, morsel by morsel.

Edmund Clayton comforted Angus by saying that he had known patients, where intense trauma had affected the brain, return to normality after a period of time. Clinging to that slight hope Angus afforded her every kindness he could, talking to her, assuring her that one day he would find Anna and they would resume the life they had once known.

But Leah showed no interest. The pupils of her eyes remained dilated. He could have been a stranger.

A week later he was away, continuing his searching. In the morning, Jasmine was in town shopping, the doctor attending a difficult childbirth and Elizabeth had slipped out to deliver some medicine to an elderly patient. Leah occupied her usual position in the chair, whimpering occasionally, for once alone.

Realizing that the house was quiet, she rose to her feet and unsteadily made her way through a door and along a corridor to the doctor's pharmacy. Its door was locked, but on a side-hideaway she found the key. Inside the pharmacy she discovered shelves filled with drugs, liniments, ointments, pain-killers, pills — and then her gaze drifted to the jars on the top shelf. In bright red lettering, they bore the word POISON.

She fetched the small step-ladder, climbed it and reached for the jar marked ARSENIC, her trembling hands nearly dropping it as she lifted it down. She was panting, her eyes rolling. She pulled off the jar's top. Inside, it was filled to the brim with white powder. She did not hesitate. She plunged her fingers into the jar and scooped the powder into her mouth — once, twice, three times. She coughed and choked but she swallowed it down, after which she dropped the jar. It smashed on the stone floor, scattering powder right across it.

When the family returned she had vomited. She was slumped in her chair, jerking her head from side to side, trying to close her mouth all the while, as if she had a heavy weight on her jaw.

With his thin, gentle hand, Doctor Clayton felt her stomach, but she shrieked with pain. Sweat was glistening on her forehead and her teeth chattered. Only when he later entered his pharmacy did he, with horror, realize what had happened. By then it was too late.

Leah died that night, despite the doctor's efforts to save her. Angus, back from his searching, was with her in the final tortuorus moments of her life, pressing her crucifix into her hands. He watched her face in the flickering lamplight, watched as she eventually grew calm and her breathing shallowed through silence-haunted moments to nothing.

The Claytons withdrew, leaving Angus to cradle her head on his lap, his fingers smoothing away the tumbled yellow hair, his jaw clamped in a tight knot.

* * *

From the time of his wife's death Angus became a changed man. His whole being dissolved into despair. His face remained brushed with the shadow of grief, the lines around his eyes creating the impression that he was viewing life from a defensive redoubt. A week or so ago he and Leah had had everything they'd wanted. Perhaps it was minimal, but it was enough to make them happy. Now black rivers of hatred flowed through him. Always serious by nature, his moods plunged to the depths, robbing him of the ability to smile. He was like a deeply wounded animal, moving within a bleak dream-world, cursed by remorse for his lack of foresight.

On a cold, stormy day, that October of 1888, Leah was buried close to Ed Mullins in the town's cemetery, where some of the wooden crosses had been tipped sideways by the scouring wind. Angus stood with his head bowed, the smell of newly turned earth in his nostrils. He twisted his hat in his hands, scarcely aware of the minister's words — scarcely aware of young Elizabeth, whose thick brown hair was caught in a graceful pony tail, her head barely reaching his shoulder. She stayed close to him, her eyes fixed on him like a dutiful daughter, trying to soften his grief.

The following week Henry Sullivan, the county sheriff, arrived in town. He was a sixty-year-old whose face was lined by the rigours of illness. He questioned Angus at length about events. He recommended to the mayor that a permanent deputy be appointed to assist the town marshal. But Angus, in his gloom, held out little hope that this measure would bring justice. The killer-cum-rapist could be far away by now, maybe he had even left the country, inflicting his cruelty elsewhere.

Meanwhile Angus went through the motions of drawing his life together. He knew that he could not impose upon the goodwill of the Clayton family for any longer. Nor did he feel he could reopen the ferry. It held too many memories and dreams that were now dead. There could be no life for him there. Instead, he rented lodgings in town. He was not a wealthy man. He needed to create some source of income. He put the ferry house and business up for sale, advertising it in the *Pawnee Bend Gazette* and through the real estate agency in town and further afield. It would prove a good business for anybody willing to work hard, but whoever took it on would have to move quickly to re-establish it before some alternative means of river crossing was established.

Angus struck up a friendship with Will Staveley, editor of the *Pawnee Bend Gazette*, who showed a great interest in the grim events that had occurred at the ferry. It was he who suggested that Angus should apply for the job of deputy town marshal. After a day or two of pondering, Angus concluded that such employment would serve two purposes: to provide a steady income and, more important, to enable him to keep ever vigilant for his enemies.

Accordingly, he went to the town marshal's office early one morning, and there found Fred Terrill reading the newspaper. He condescended to lower the newspaper, but made no effort to straighten up.

'I understand there's a vacancy for deputy marshal,' Angus said.

Terrill shook his head. 'Not now there ain't.'

'How's that?'

Terrill coughed, showing reluctance to explain further. 'Made an appointment yesterday.' He picked up the newspaper as if the conversation had been concluded.

Angus persisted. 'Who got the job?'

Terrill remained hidden behind the newspaper. He clicked his teeth.

'Johnny Kypp,' he said.

11

Three days later, The *Pawnee Bend Gazette* carried the story:

After reviewing several applications for the appointment, Town Marshal Frederick Terrill selected former outlaw John H. Kypp for the job of his deputy. Kypp, an experienced gunslinger, is now a reformed character, having served his time in jail, and Terrill has convinced the town council that he will provide the necessary toughness and dedication that the post demands. Kypp is currently recovering from an injury received in a family altercation, but should be fit to assume his duties within a fortnight.

Angus was astounded. But gradually he realized that there was no legal reason why Kypp should not be appointed. Only in Angus's mind was he guilty. As he adjusted to the idea he saw that at last he would have the opportunity to confront Kypp. This he welcomed. Here was the enemy he had been hunting, the man who had shot Ed Mullins and raped his wife — or so he had persuaded himself to believe. Now that hunt might well be over.

He kept a careful watch on the marshal's office over the next two weeks, his eyes aching for sight of Kypp. Meanwhile, Edmund Clayton offered him a job as assistant in his pharmacy.

'But I don't know the first thing about medicines,' Angus argued.

Clayton gave him his thin smile. 'You don't need to. All you'll have to do is package them up and deliver them around town. Anyway, Elizabeth will give you a hand.'

Angus thought about it, then nodded. At least it would provide him with a small income for the time being and he had always prided himself on being a quick learner.

On the day following his commence-ment of work at the pharmacy he was approached by a stranger in town, a German called Franz Kruger, who said he was interested in buying the ferry house and business. Kruger was a thickset, pugnacious man, but he seemed genuine enough. He and his family had recently immigrated from Hamburg. After negotiation, and Kruger's further inspection of the property, the German offered a sum slightly lower than the asking price. Angus accepted, the deal was agreed and the necessary legal documents completed and witnessed by Pawnee Bend's attorney.

Kruger also purchased the draught-horses, pony and wagon. When all the money was paid and lodged in the bank, Angus had the satisfaction of being financially solvent — at least for the time being. But what good was money when all the happiness had been torn from his life?

After he had cleared out from the house the few items that he wished to keep he handed the keys to the new owner with a heavy heart. He regretted that the ferry was no longer the responsibility of a Troon, having been built and run by father and son for so many years, but his regrets were immediately dwarfed into insignificance by the other sorrows branded into his memory.

He would never escape the conviction that he had failed his wife and child; he recalled the sweetness of Leah's smile, how the sun glinted in her gold hair; how she radiated love. He was thankful that Old Man Havelock, who had entrusted him with the lovely flower of his daughter, was not alive to know how that flower had been crushed in terrible death.

Late one evening, in the following month, when Angus was returning to town after delivering some medicines to an outlying ranch, he met Will Staveley.

'Thought you'd like to know,' the

newspaper editor confided. 'Johnny Kypp has taken up his appointment with Fred Terrill. So far as I know, he's over in the office now.'

Angus tensed. It was as if his heart had been seized in an icy grip.

Staveley reached out to lay a restraining hand on his arm. 'You'd better tread carefully, Angus. Maybe Kypp's guilty of causing your troubles, maybe he isn't. But one thing's certain. He's a tough and violent man and no stranger to using a gun.'

Angus's breathing had quickened. He nodded. 'He must know something, that's for sure.'

Grim-faced, he returned to his lodgings and strapped on his Navy Colt, caressing the trigger with his finger. Images of Leah's final moments filled his mind. The way her tongue had protruded from her mouth; her lungs heaving; her eyes like luminous globes; the death-rattle. He slipped five rounds into the gun's chamber and holstered it at his hip. He would make Johnny Kypp pay for his part in what had happened. If he was subsequently accused of murder, he would face the penalty willingly.

★   ★   ★

Darkness was taking hold as he strode purposefully up the street towards the marshal's office. The cold air brought a shiver to his spine. The sidewalks were quiet, the stores closed. The only sound came from the saloon: the desultory notes of a Tin-Panny piano, the raucous voices of men, the shrill laugh of a woman. He felt certain he heard Terrill's slurred speech.

Leah had once told Angus that nothing was achieved by violence, but now he was convinced that she'd been wrong. The desire to inflict vengeance brought the bitter taste of bile to his mouth. However, before bullets started flying, he had to get the truth from Johnny Kypp.

Coming abreast the law office he

paused on the opposite sidewalk. A couple of horses were hitched to the outside rail. One of them was Kypp's Morgan. A lantern glowed from within the office and the door stood slightly ajar. He drew his gun from its holster, the firmness of the butt in his hand reinforcing his determination; then he crossed the wide, rutted street and mounted the sidewalk. A second later he pushed open the door and stepped inside.

He was met by the stench of cheap perfume, and with it the sound of a woman's ecstatic groans. His eyes were drawn to the female back, moving sinuously and clothed in the bright red of a hurdy-gurdy girl. She was perched on the front of the marshal's desk, her skirts drawn up to reveal frilly garters and the tops of black silk stockings, her legs astride the man slumped in the chair beneath her. Her hands were cupping his face, her lips feeding off his with the desperation akin to a starving wolf.

The unexpected scene took Angus aback, halting him in his tracks. He was unable to see the man so encompassed by this voracious female, whom he recognized. She was known as 'Squirrel Tooth' Sally, a girl from 'the palace of sinful pleasure' — a well-soiled dove.

Suddenly Sally became aware that they were not alone; she drew back her lips and turned her rouge-cheeked face around, indignation flaring in her eyes. But Angus was more interested in the now-revealed man who was struggling to regain some composure. Angus was desperately trying to fit the face of Johnny Kypp on to the individual's shoulders — but could not. He slowly came to terms with the fact that this was not the man he sought. He was Dave Sangster, one of Marshal Terrill's part-time deputies, a youngster who provided his services once or twice a week to help preserve law and order in the town — but he had a strange way of doing it.

The woman slid down from the desk, smoothing her dress into place.

'Ain't no cause for you to look so shocked, Angus Troon,' she said. ''Specially after all them tricks you used to get up to before you married that prissy . . . '

Angus silenced her with an angry glare and she trailed off, suddenly afraid of him. She was right of course; he'd been as guilty as any other woman-lusting male.

Sangster stood up, hastily buttoning his jeans. 'Weren't expectin' no callers,' he said. 'What d'you want?'

Angus glanced around, satisfying himself that there was nobody else in the office or adjoining cell.

'I want Johnny Kypp,' he said. 'I heard he's taken up his duties.'

'He has,' Sangster grunted. He chose to overcome his embarrassment with arrogance. 'What d'you want with Deputy Kypp?'

'I need to pay off a debt,' Angus replied.

Sangster hesitated, his eyes glancing over Angus's shoulder through the window, then he said, 'He's patrollin' the town, keepin' law and order like he's paid to do. You best put that gun away, otherwise you'll get arrested for breakin' the peace.'

Angus shifted his position, moving away from the open door. Silhouetted in the lighted room he would have been a clear target. He slipped his gun into its holster.

'If Johnny Kypp comes back here,' he said, 'tell him that Angus Troon is looking for him.'

Turning, he stepped from the office on to the sidewalk; the thought that Kypp was somewhere out here, drifting through the darkened streets, quickened his pulse. The town seemed dead, apart from the saloon.

In the shadows beneath the covered way he paused, his gaze probing the gloom. Further along light was spilling out from the saloon, revealing the numerous horses hitched to the rail outside. Even at a distance he concluded that proceedings were getting somewhat riotous. He knew that a bunch of cowboys had ridden in from the ranges that afternoon and were no doubt splashing their money around on liquor and fancy women. If the steadying hand of the law was needed anywhere, it was probably in the bar room. Maybe Kypp was there. Angus grunted with disbelief. It was crazy that an outlaw like Kypp was masquerading as a lawman.

He crossed the street. Pacing through the shadows, he peered warily into the darkened alleyways. He was conscious that at any moment he might encounter the man he hated.

He remembered the saloon well enough, even the hurdy-gurdy girls, from the wild days before Leah had brought sobriety to his life. Then, he'd sworn that he'd never touch the low life again. Now Leah was gone and he knew he was a bitter man, his ambition narrowed to nothing beyond vengeance.

He would not rest until another man was in his grave.

As he neared the saloon he realized that the voices and commotion he heard were not the drunken, light-hearted banter of cowboys. Hard, threatening words were being exchanged.

He passed a man sitting on the sidewalk, his hands holding an undoubtedly sore head. He did not look up as Angus stepped by.

He reached the pool of light outside the door of the saloon, surprised by the increasing ferocity of the bar-room voices. Then he braced himself and entered the crowded place, pressing his back against the inside wall. As his eyes adjusted to the light, he was stunned by the view thus afforded.

12

The long room was lit by a multitude of kerosene lamps, the whole place thick with tobacco smoke, reeking with alcohol and there was an unmistakable tension in the air. It showed in men's eyes. Some loud-mouthed cowpunchers had grouped at one end of the bar. One of them Angus knew of old. He was a troublemaker called Bradshaw. He had unholstered his six-shooter, was waving it in the air.

Then Angus became aware of another man — standing close to a felt-topped table. Here some gamblers had been playing poker, but now they paused, looking up, white-faced. The nearby man was wearing a cartridge belt with a six-gun. His cheeks were scarred by pockmarks, his hair was braided Indian-fashion and there was a deputy's star pinned to his shirt.

Angus's blood turned to ice, knowing that at this moment he had the drop on Kypp because he was unaware of his presence. He could kill him with a single bullet and all his troubles would be over — or would they?

But suddenly Kypp's voice prodded firmly into the loaded atmosphere. 'I told you. No gunplay in here. Put that gun away.'

Bradshaw made no effort to comply. A insolent smile spread across his pug-nosed features. 'Ain't no jumped-up bank-robber givin' me orders! You should be back in jail, where you belong.'

Kypp did not to flinch; he just radiated cold, deadly venom. 'I give you one more warnin',' he hissed. 'You put that gun away or you're a corpse!'

Bradshaw was about to respond with further abuse, but another man spoke. Fred Terrill had stumbled to his feet, knocking over his chair in the process. Angus realized that he had been slumped across a table, obviously in a drunken stupor, but now he had drawn his gun. His words came in a slur. 'You do as . . . my dep-deputy says, Bradshaw. Kypp's served his sentence for the crime he c-committed. He's as innocent as you now!'

Bradshaw's response stabbed across the room. 'Go to hell, Terrill!'

The marshal's inebriated eyes contorted with anger. He swung his gun in Bradshaw's direction and pulled the trigger. The bullet struck the wall above the cowboy's head, scattering a shower of plaster. But as the room reverberated with blast and the accompanying screams and shouts, another shot roared out. Terrill was thrown backwards on to the sawdust floor, splintering a table, his shirt-front showing an explosion of blood, his face growing purple as he struggled to draw oxygen into his lungs.

Across the room men scattered to avoid further bullets and the barkeeps ducked down. Bradshaw stood alone, gun in hand, a shroud of smoke hanging about him.

'Self-defence,' he shouted out. 'He'd've killed me otherwise!'

Johnny Kypp ran forward, fell to his knees alongside Terrill's body. 'He ain't dead,' he yelled out. 'He's still breathin'. We gotta get him to the doctor's.' He glanced around, for the first time meeting Angus's cold stare. He hesitated, his eyes widening, then said: 'Don't just stand there. Give me a hand!'

Angus was aware of men rushing towards the door; they moved so fast a swarm of bees could have been chasing them. One cowboy brushed him aside as he departed. It was Bradshaw.

'Give me a dawgone hand!' Kypp repeated angrily.

Scarcely realizing what he was doing, Angus stepped across to the sprawled frame of Fred Terrill, seeing how the lawman's chin was stained with a dark froth he'd coughed up and how the surrounding floor was shining with the blood that soaked into the sawdust. He needed medical attention — fast. Angus stooped down, grabbed the marshal beneath the armpits.

'Let's get him to Doc Clayton's,' he said. 'His place is close.'

Kypp nodded and took hold of the marshal's legs.

Angus felt the crazy unreality of what was happening, but he went on with it although Kypp's nearness had his nerves hammering.

Together they raised Terrill's leaden weight and carried him out through the door. The saloon's customers had vanished with surprising speed.

Angus nodded down the street and they carried their burden along the sidewalk, exchanging no words. Angus was relieved to see that a light was burning in the doctor's surgery. They rested the weight down and he pounded on the door. A flushed Elizabeth opened up, her young face wincing as she saw the reason for their visit. Behind her was the beanpole figure of her father. Within a minute,

Terrill had been placed on the surgery table.

With his long fingers Clayton pulled back the gory shirt from the wound. He shook his head.

'The bullet's gone deep,' he said, 'maybe punctured his lung. I'll try to get it out, but I can't guarantee he'll survive. Who did it?'

'Bradshaw,' Angus said, aware of Johnny Kypp's brooding gaze resting on him. He avoided the man's eyes.

'Serious matter, shooting a law officer,' Clayton said, picking small pieces of sodden cloth from Terrill's flesh, then he turned to Elizabeth. 'Get me some boiling water quick as you can.' She nodded and rushed to comply.

'You gentlemen best leave him in my hands now,' the doctor went on, working with his scissors. 'I'll do what I can.'

Kypp grunted his acknowledgement. Angus exchanged a look with the doctor. He followed Kypp out on to the street, his mind in a turmoil from the way his immediate intentions had been sidetracked.

Once on the sidewalk Kypp stopped walking and swung around, his frame silhouetted by moonlight, his brooding eyes in pools of shadow. Angus braced himself, resting his hand on the butt of his gun.

'Johnny Kypp,' he said, 'you know me and I know you. We can cut out the formalities. My wife's dead, my partner murdered, my child vanished . . . and my life ruined. I hold you guilty and I aim to make you pay.'

Kypp sucked in breath, then he spat out his words, 'If it hadn't been for you, we'd never have been shut away in that stinkin' hole of a prison. I'd never done wrong before, but nobody took that to account when they dished out those sentences.'

'You got what you deserved,' Angus countered, his voice rising, 'and it doesn't seem you learned your lesson. Kypp, maybe it was your first crime but you still broke the law and that wasn't my fault. And now you're here, pretending to uphold the law. But you can't fool me!'

If Kypp had grabbed for his gun at that moment Angus would have done likewise, hurled himself to the side and blasted off, but Kypp made no sudden movement. Instead, he said, 'You're crazy.' And then the tension seemed to flow out of him and he added: 'If it's your kid you're concerned about, I may be able to help.'

'What!' Angus could scarcely believe his ears. 'She . . . she's still alive?'

Kypp's braided head moved ever so slightly. It could have been a nod or a shake.

'Come over to the office tomorrow about . . . say about three in the afternoon,' he said, 'I'll have other business to see to first. I might, just might, have something to tell you.'

He turned away, as if inviting a bullet in his broad back. Angus stood motionless, stunned, watching him walk steadily up the street to the marshal's office. With Fred Terrill sidelined for clearly a long time, or maybe for ever, Johnny Kypp was now the chief representative of the law in Pawnee Bend. The situation seemed beyond belief.

Angus bridled his frustration. The man's words lingered in his ears. Maybe it was just some cruel taunt, his way of increasing Angus's suffering. On the other hand, could this be the first real hope he'd had since Anna had disappeared?

Some impulse had Angus glancing back at the Claytons' house. He saw Elizabeth gazing from a window. Her face looked like that of a delicate porcelain doll. She waved to him and he waved back.

He returned to his lodgings, anxious for the morrow to come. The possibility that Anna might still be alive made his heart pound and gave him a restless night. Maybe Kypp considered that his revenge for being shut away in jail had been completed — or maybe taking on the job as lawman in Pawnee Bend was some sort of cover-up for future wrong-doings.

Whatever Kypp's motives, Angus couldn't trust the man. He must watch him with the intensity of a bird of prey. But if Kypp could get little Anna back for him, and she was unharmed, then he might be able to find some reconciliation in his heart. One thing was certain, it wasn't in his interest to kill the man right now.

★ ★ ★

Next morning he rose early. Winter was casting its bleak mantle upon the land. He took breakfast at a café but didn't have much of an appetite. He wondered how he would find the reserve and patience to wait for the afternoon to arrive. Kypp had been strangely specific about the time of the appointment at his office.

When he arrived at the Clayton

pharmacy for his morning's work Elizabeth opened the door, her usual gentle smile absent.

'Angus,' she greeted him, 'you've heard?'

'No . . . what?'

'Fred Terrill died last night. Dad tried his hardest to save him, but the bullet had gone through his lungs.'

Angus shook his head gloomily. He'd never been an admirer of the town's marshal, for he'd been a perpetual drinker and gambler, doing little to gain the respect that was necessary for his job. But for any man to lose his life in this way was bad news.

'Did he have any family?' Angus enquired.

The girl shook her head. 'He was a loner. Maybe way back he had a wife, but nobody knows. Dad sent a note across to Johnny Kypp, saying he'd better arrest Bradshaw on a charge of murder. He also went over and told Mayor Henry. The mayor said he was appointing Kypp as town marshal.'

Angus drew a deep, fretful breath and stepped into the pharmacy to commence his work.

All morning and during the early afternoon, he watched the clock inch away the minutes, the hours. It seemed the longest day he'd ever known. At last the hands pointed to five minutes before three. He strapped on his gun, having carefully thumbed five cartridges into the loading gate. He left the pharmacy and walked briskly along the street towards the marshal's office, ignoring the inquisitive stares of several ladies who stood with their skirts hoisted above the mud. The time of truth was nigh — or so he hoped.

13

He found the door of the office closed, no movement showing from within. He recalled last time he had been to the place. Kypp hadn't been there, now he hoped he was waiting for him — not with a gun in his hand, but with news of hope. On the other hand, was he walking into some fiendish trap?

His grip closed over the knob, pushing the door open. If the place had looked deserted from the outside, he now found that it was not. A wizened, stumpy man was sitting with his bandy legs on the cluttered desk. He looked up bleary-eyed from his doze as the visitor entered, the knife-scars on his cheeks looking angry, his lolling mouth revealing a mass of blackened stubs.

He was Linus Kypp, Johnny's dwarf of a father. His eyes narrowed as he recognized Angus and he made no form of greeting. The hostility he radiated was reciprocated by Angus.

'Johnny said you'd most likely call in,' old Linus announced, speaking as if the production of words pained his mouth. 'God a'mighty, I hoped I'd never set eyes on you again.'

'Where is he — Johnny?' Angus demanded.

The old man feigned an indifferent attitude. He spat out a stream of brown liquid, missing the spittoon. He picked a shred of tobacco from the tip of his tongue with dirty fingers, taking an irritating length of time before answering.

'As soon as he heard 'bout Marshal Terrill havin' died,' he said, 'he set out to arrest his killer. Reckoned he'd be back before you got here, but it ain't so. Maybe Bradshaw has objected to being arrested.'

Angus sighed with frustration. 'Did he ask you to pass on a message to me — anything?'

'Nothin',' Linus Kypp grunted,

enjoying the game he was playing. 'Johnny and me have just resumed speakin' terms.'

Angus felt like grabbing the old man around the neck like a scraggy hen, shaking him until he was more informative, but he resisted the temptation.

'Why are you here, anyway?' he grunted.

'Life got kinda miserable at home,' Linus Kypp said. 'Couldn't stand it no longer. All your dawgone fault, mind.'

'My fault — why!'

'My woman, Arabella. She said I'd not treated Johnny the way a father should treat his son. Just 'cos I told him he wasn't worth a pinch of dried owl-shit. She said I should come and make things up with him, 'specially since he's taken up this deputy job. 'Course he never guessed he'd become full blown town marshal himself, which he now is. Mayor handed him the badge first thing this mornin'.'

'You said it was my fault, all this

trouble at home,' Angus persisted.

'Angus Troon,' Kypp said, fresh anger bringing a flush to his cheeks, 'if you hadn't yapped off your mouth at that trial, Johnny would never have gone to jail. Furthermore, our family name would never have been dragged into the shit. That's something I can never forgive!'

'But why should that make you hard on Johnny?' Angus asked in exasperation.

Kypp licked the dried flakes of skin that were his lips.

'Guess I've talked too much,' he grunted. 'Guess I should've kept my mouth shut.'

'Just tell me!' Angus shouted.

Kypp turned his head, gazed out into the street, no doubt wishing his son would return and get him out of the apparent hole he was digging for himself. His eyes swung back to Angus.

'Truth is,' he went on, 'I got real angry with Johnny. Told him to get out of our home. I told him he'd gone soft on you, that he owed it to me to make your life hell until Duquemain came out of jail and finished the job off. Yes, I kicked him out of our place, told him never to come back. That's exactly what he tried to do, but as soon as I saw him I fired a couple o' shots in his direction, not meanin' to hit him, mind you. Just to let him know he weren't welcome. Never thought his horse would rear up that way, throw him off and hurt his leg.'

Things were becoming clearer to Angus now. 'It was just after I called on you, wasn't it?'

Linus Kypp nodded. 'That's why I was so damned riled up. It was you I should have fired at. Ever since, Arabella's gone on at me, like as if she's got a viper in her mouth — on and on and on. 'You should say sorry to poor Johnny. You ain't no right to treat your boy that way!' She nigh whipped me out of my own home with her doggone tongue.'

Angus was growing tired of the man's

rambling, but at least things made more sense now.

'You said Johnny was too soft with me,' he said. 'What did you mean?'

Kypp hesitated, then his mouth opened to speak, but at that moment they both heard a commotion from outside. Kypp stood up and joined Angus at the window.

Excited men were swarming like summer flies about the rider who had just reined-in his Morgan outside the office. Across the saddle of his horse was a body fastened on with a rope. Angus knew immediately that here was the corpse of the cowboy, Bradshaw — murderer of Marshal Terrill.

Angus rushed to the doorway and stepped out on to the sidewalk. The crowd was increasing, unleashing shouts of congratulation.

'Thank God we got law in town again!'

'Well done, Johnny!'

'Saved us the cost of lynchin' the devil!'

Johnny Kypp acknowledged their shouts with a nod. Still in the saddle, he unfastened the rope and allowed Bradshaw's body to slide to the ground. It landed in a ungainly heap.

'Take him away,' he shouted out. 'Take him to the morgue and put him alongside Fred Terrill so he can see that justice has been done.'

There were several assenting cries, then numerous hands reached down to take hold of the corpse and convey it across the street to James Hammond's Funeral Parlour. Angus noticed that Bradshaw had been shot in the back — and at close range because his shirt was powder-blackened. Meanwhile, Johnny Kypp dismounted, hitched his horse to the rail, climbed the steps to the sidewalk — and came face to face with Angus.

Angus did not waste time. 'You said you had news about my child,' he said. 'Where is she?'

Kypp had had a half-smile on his face; now that disappeared. It seemed

157

he intended to ignore the question because he reached out to brush Angus aside and continue on into the office.

'I'm busy right now,' he commented from the side of his mouth. 'I got paperwork to fill in.'

'Damn you, Kypp,' Angus snapped out. 'Quit playing games. Just tell me what you know!'

'You let Johnny be,' another voice snarled, 'or I'll shoot you where you stand!'

Both Angus and Johnny turned to see old Linus Kypp standing in the doorway, the heavy artillery of his .50-calibre Sharps in his hands.

Johnny nodded to his father, then continued to walk into his office. At that point Angus was unable to restrain his fury. He threw himself at Johnny Kypp, intent on twisting him around, but instead his weight plunged against his back, catapulting him forward into his father. Both men went down in a sprawling heap blocking the doorway. In the confusion Linus's gun exploded with a deafemng roar. Johnny rolled aside, turning the air blue with curses, his shirt-sleeve showing the burn of gunpowder, the air thick with sulphur fumes.

Angus immediately drew his own Navy Colt, covering the two fallen men. He could hear footsteps and shouting sounding in the street behind him, folks coming to see what was going on.

'Where's my child?' Angus shouted. 'Tell me!'

The younger Kypp was stunned, but he found himself gazing into Angus's gun. He glared at his father, who himself was sitting up, wincing with the pain the fall had caused, wincing with the embarrassment of having nearly blown his son's head off, this not fitting his current inclination.

Johnny Kypp was seething with anger, his hand to his wounded arm. 'Damn you, Pa,' he cried. 'Never could aim straight!'

'I'm sorry, Johnny. It was the way I fell.'

In his anger, Angus's finger tightened on his trigger, sent a bullet whipping into the sidewalk a few inches from where Johnny had fallen.

'I won't ask you again,' he snarled. 'Where's my child?'

Johnny Kypp had flinched as the shot thudded close to him. For the first time a brief fear showed in his eyes. Instinct warned him that he was seconds away from another bullet, and next time Angus would aim to kill.

His eyes flickered towards his father. 'You better tell him, Pa. You tell him the truth.'

Linus cursed. 'Can't do that, Johnny. I promised Arabella.'

Johnny Kypp gazed at Angus. 'You got no cause to hate me, Troon. I never did you no harm, well not much, anyway.'

Angus flexed his gun, his finger taking up the trigger slack, his patience exhausted. 'The child . . . or you die!' and he meant it. Johnny knew that.

'Tell him, Pa,' he repeated, his tone

desperate. His arm was paining him. 'Tell him!' The whole situation had turned sour for him.

Old man Kypp hesitated, cursed again and drew the back of his hand across his dribbling lips. 'Arabella will never forgive me for this,' he muttered. 'She's taken to that kid like her own, ever since Glaswall brought it in . . .'

'The child's at your place?' Angus demanded.

The old man's nod was almost imperceptible.

'Who's Glaswall?'

At that moment other men had joined them, enquiring what was going on. Somebody grabbed Angus's arm, but he shook himself free. He had no time to explain: let the Kypps do that. He holstered his gun, turned and strode away. The incandescent glow of hope was burning inside him. Little Anna was alive . . . *alive!*

14

A powdery snow was falling as he went to the livery to fetch Judas, but everywhere was locked up and there was a note pinned to the door saying *Back five minutes. Abe Simmons.*

He tried the door. It was firmly bolted. Five minutes came and went, became ten, then twenty. Angus cursed. He debated whether he should kick the door down, but decided to check the saloon for Abe Simmons first. When he entered, a few of the drinkers looked up.

'Where's Abe?' he enquired. 'I need my horse.'

One man nodded towards the upper floor. 'Better ask Squirrel Tooth Sally,' he grinned.

Angus grunted with impatience and went and sat on the bottom stair, hoping Simmons was shortly to come down. He kept hearing the high-pitched laughter of Sally coming from upstairs. It seemed that she and her guest were nowhere near reaching a culminating moment. He decided to wait no longer. He returned to the livery. It took half a dozen hefty kicks to force a panel out of the door. And thereafter it was easy to reach up inside and slide the bolt back.

As he was getting a saddle across Judas's back, Elizabeth Clayton entered the livery. He quickly told her what had occurred.

'I'll come with you, Angus,' she stated.

'No,' he said firmly. 'It'll be too dangerous.'

'But you'll need somebody to look after Anna.'

'No, Elizabeth. I appreciate your offer, but no, no, no! Your dad would never forgive me if anything bad happened. Go on home.'

He saw the hurt moisten her eyes.

He climbed into his saddle and heeled the sorrel through the livery doorway into the street. He glanced over his shoulder, saw Elizabeth's slight figure and her face awash with disappointment — but he was sure he'd done the right thing. He gave her a wave.

He looked up the street towards the marshal's office. The crowd had dispersed. He wondered what lies Johnny Kypp and his old man had told. He dismissed them from his mind. He had the most important business in the world to attend to.

The wind was getting up, the cold biting into him as he rode but he did not care. His entire body was throbbing with excitement. If only Leah could be with him. Thought of her started a circle of pain in his belly. Maybe the joy of finding her lovely babe would have restored her sanity, but now he must act for both of them.

He kept Judas at a brisk trot, skirting the out-of-town homesteads and shadowed forest before moving northward into the series of sprawling valleys, signs of civilization fading behind him. He reckoned it would take him a couple of hours to reach Kelly's Hole. Another twenty minutes would see him at the Kypps's wretched homestead.

Only once, when he looked back, did he imagine that he saw a rider on the trail far behind him, but later, when he crossed over higher ground, a further glance revealed nothing to arouse his attention, apart from the flapping of a distant crow. The image of Anna's little face, her blue eyes, her fair hair, so like her mother's, remained in his mind.

He recalled how the little family had sometimes picnicked in the grass, with the sun shining and the flowers smelling so sweetly. *Oh, Leah, if only you could be with me now on the way to reclaim our lives.* And he felt tears on his cheeks, brushed them away. He rode, revelling in the warmth of his memories, bending low in the saddle so that the brim of his hat deflected the snow from his eyes.

So immersed in his thoughts was he

that he was hardly aware of how the day had darkened, how the temperature had plunged even lower. It was growing gloomier by the minute, but the excitement within him pounded. How would Anna have changed over the weeks since she had been snatched from her family? Had she been injured at all? Had she cried for her mama and papa? So many questions.

And then Judas stumbled into the rope strung across the trail!

It had been no more than an evil eighteen inches above the ground, nigh invisible, stretched taut, enough to have the horse somersaulting and Angus flying from his saddle. He was dimly aware of hitting the ground with a bone-jarring impact, landing on his left shoulder and everything seeming to whirl about. He was stunned, convinced that he was terribly injured. For the moment, all he could do was remain still, unable to restrain his groaning, dimly aware of Judas stomping and snorting off to the side and of snow coming down — and pain, hard pain, throbbing through him. He wondered if his back was broken.

And then he heard footsteps shuffling towards him, and something poked him roughly in the side. It was a dwarf-sized boot.

'Still alive then,' Linus Kypp's voice crackled. 'Was hopin' you might've cracked your damn skull open. Then you'd have been done for. Everybody would've figured you'd been thrown by your horse.'

Angus was beginning to sort his brain out, shaking his head to dispel the daze.

'I've had to wait out here a long time in the snow,' Kypp went on. 'Thought you was never gonna show up. I wasn't gonna let you outfox me again, though.'

'What are you after?' Angus gasped. He tried to move, to raise himself up, but his back hurt too much.

He had no clear view of the old man; he was standing behind him, but he knew he had his big rifle trained on him; he could smell its oil.

'First thing,' Kypp said, 'is that you'll never take that kid from Arabella. She'll never give it up. She absolutely dotes on it. It would kill her if you snatched it away, and she'd take it out on me, that's for sure. Anyway, she looks after it a darned sight better'n than you would.'

Angus tried to move again and got his shoulders slightly off the ground. This situation was crazy.

'How did she get hold of her?' he managed to ask.

He heard Kypp spit. 'Glaswall knew she was down-right broody, said he'd get her a baby, seeing her husband couldn't oblige.'

'Glaswall?' Angus gasped. 'Who's he?'

The old man snarled with impatience. 'If anybody knows Silas Glaswall, you should!'

'Well, I don't. Who the hell is he?'

'Thanks to your big mouth,' Linus Kypp explained, 'he got shut away in prison along with Johnny. He got five years as well. He got set free with Johnny.'

Recollection of Glaswall was filtering into Angus's dazed mind. Glaswall had been Duquemain's second-in-command.

'Glaswall said he'd get Arabella a baby to repay us for accommodatin' him. More likely he was trying to bribe her into opening her legs for him. He was with Johnny at first, when they got out of prison, you see. Then we had the big bust-up and I told Johnny to get out, wouldn't let him back. Arabella said I was too harsh on him, nagged me to hell. Maybe she was right. But now we got some talkin' to do, some bargainin'. That's if you want to stay alive.'

Angus could sense testiness increasing in the old man.

'So what do you plan to do?' Angus spoke slowly, trying to calm him and formulate some plan to extract himself from the threat of the gun. But options seemed limited.

'I guess I don't have any choice, Mr

Angus Troon. You've been a right pain ever since Johnny and his pals crossed on your ferry, blackening the name of Kypp like you have. Anyway, you won't do it no more!'

Angus was suddenly conscious of Kypp's breathing, conscious of the fact that it would take a mere second for his finger to tighten on his trigger.

'I got an offer to make you,' Kypp wheezed.

'What offer?'

'You wanna live?'

'Just so long as I can wring your neck!' Angus grunted.

'Well, I'll tell you what. I'll offer you good money for that kid. I'm not a poor man, neither will you be if you take up this offer, clear out and leave us alone. The child won't want for anythin'. Arabella loves her crazy. I'll give you hard cash on the nail. You name the price.'

'Go to hell!' Angus said.

Elizabeth Clayton, having disregarded Angus's advice to remain behind, had been watching, biding her time, until alerted by the pandemonium of Judas's tumble. Now she spoke up with all the forceful urgency that her young voice could muster.

'Drop your gun, Mr Kypp. I've got you in my aim and I can shoot you dead.'

Angus heard Kypp's vicious profanity. There was an awful moment when nothing seemed to happen, while the old man's brain was ticking over as fast as a newly wound clock.

'Drop it, Mr Kypp.' The girl's voice came again. 'You've got five seconds. One, two, three . . . '

Kypp's gun thudded down into the snow.

Gritting his teeth against the pain, Angus heaved himself to his feet. He drew his Navy Colt and thumbed back the hammer, standing unsteadily but aiming it true at the crouched figure of the man who now appeared as the pitiful dwarf he was.

'Put your hands up,' Angus demanded.

Cursing, the old man complied.

It was then that the girl appeared, stepping out from the trees like a descending angel. Angus had never in any way associated her gentle nature with guns, nor did he have any cause to now. She held nothing in her hands but a short branch.

Kypp noticed too and unleashed an angry howl. Angus was recovering from his fall, was not lowering his guard against the old scoundrel for a moment — but his voice came gratefully.

'Elizabeth, I told you not to come out here, but I'm beholden that you did. Thanks.'

'I was so scared,' she murmured, the firmness having left her tone. 'I was so scared he'd shoot you.'

'I was only bluffin',' Kypp muttered, but Angus was not convinced.

'Elizabeth,' Angus said, keeping his eyes and gun on Kypp. With his free hand, he reached into his pocket and extracted a pocket knife. 'Cut a good length of rope from that trip-line.'

Obediently the girl took the knife; with trembling hands she opened it out.

'Don't cut the rope,' Kypp pleaded. 'It's the best rope I ever had.' Angus ignored his plea.

'Cut the rope,' he repeated, and when she had done it, he said; 'Hold the gun. Keep it pointed at him, and if he tries anything, you shoot him. I really mean that.'

Elizabeth nodded. She was in a highly agitated state, violence and threats not being part of her gentle nature, but she was being incredibly brave. She took the Navy Colt and with both hands held it aligned with Kypp.

Stepping carefully, making sure not to get between the muzzle of the gun and its possible target, Angus had the old man lower his hands, and he wound the rope around his body, binding his arms to his sides. All the while, Kypp was chuntering with frustrated fury, but soon he was quite helpless.

'Keep him covered, Elizabeth,' Angus said. 'Where's your horse?'

'Tethered back in the trees,' she responded.

'I'll catch Judas,' he said, 'then we'll ride on for the homestead. And, Elizabeth . . . '

'Yes?'

'I'm real grateful for what you did.'

Angus limped away and found his sorrel standing in the shelter of the tree. The animal was trembling and skittish, showing the whites of his eyes, but from a quick feel of his legs Angus was pretty sure that the fall had not seriously injured him. The same went for himself, he concluded thankfully, though his body was probably black and blue.

Linus explained that he had a horse, tethered not far away. Angus sent Elizabeth away to release it and fetch her own, which she had done within five minutes. Kypp's animal could find its own way home. Angus had no intention of letting the old man ride. Let him stumble along!

174

15

It was well after midnight when they eventually reached the run-down dwelling that was the Kypps's residence. They had ridden in grim silence, battling against wind and snow. A light shone from the window. They reined in their tired animals on the slope fronting the place. The old man was exhausted and totally dispirited. Angus had showed him no mercy, forcing him to stumble on. But now Angus felt invigorated by the knowledge that he might be on the threshold of reclaiming Anna. He was mighty grateful that Elizabeth had come along despite his reluctance for her to do so. My God, he had ample reason to be!

Linus Kypp had slumped to the muddy ground; his legs had finally given out. It seemed he couldn't care less what happened next, but Angus didn't trust him one iota.

Angus cupped his hands to his mouth and called: 'Hullo there!'

The response was a twitching of the curtain, a movement of the lantern from inside, then the door opened and the slim figure of Arabella Kypp appeared, drawing a shawl about her shoulders. She was holding the lantern.

'Who is there?' she enquired anxiously.

'It's Angus Troon. We won't harm you if you do as you're told.'

'Oh . . .'

'Stay here, Elizabeth,' he said, lowering his voice. 'Keep your eye on the old man.'

She murmured her understanding as he slipped from his saddle. His body still ached all over, but expectation had him quickly moving down the slope into the brighter circle of Arabella Kypp's lantern.

'Are you alone?' he demanded.

Arabella hesitated, then said: '*Sí*. Where's Linus?'

He noticed how her dark hair was flattened and wet. She must have been outside recently.

'Linus is resting for a moment,' he explained. 'He's had a long walk. Give me the light.'

He took the lantern from her hand and walked straight past her and into the cabin. Many unwholesome smells assailed his nostrils, but one was more distinctive than the others. It was *baby*.

The whole place was a tip; everything was littered about and filthy-looking. Half-finished food, dirty dishes, cast-off clothing, muddy boots. Even the pictures on the wall were hanging crooked. There were three small rooms, leading off what stood for the parlour — and the full, insistent cry of a child led him to the third. He saw a cot against the far wall and he could hardly breathe with emotion.

'Leave the baby,' Arabella cried from behind him. ''Tis not yours!'

Angus ignored her, unable to stop the name of Anna from coming to his lips.

He placed the lantern on a table. He reached into the cradle and drew the child out, his heart hammering, his gaze centering on its small face, its mouth open as it screamed with fear. He struggled to mould the child's reddened features into those of Anna. It took him twenty seconds before he was totally convinced. And then the dreadful truth dawned on him.

This was not his child.

'Where's my Anna?' he shouted above the bawl. 'Where's my baby?

'I told you,' Arabella said. ''Tis not yours. I do not know about your *chica*.'

'You're lying,' he snapped out, but she stood, hands on hips, shaking her dark head from side to side.

'I know nothing of your *chica*.'

He returned the struggling baby to its cradle and Arabella stepped past him, picked it up and hugged it against her breast, gradually soothing its cries.

He felt devastated. He wanted to weep with frustration, with disappointment. He paced the room clenching and unclenching his fists.

'Where's Glaswall?' he shouted at last. 'He must know where Anna is!'

'Glaswall?' she murmured vaguely. 'He has not been here for a long time.'

He stamped through the cabin. He climbed the slope to where Elizabeth still sat her horse and Linus lay upon the snowy ground.

Angus reached down, grabbed the old man by the shoulders. 'I thought you said my child was here!'

Linus groaned. Angus shook him really hard.

'I'm an old man,' he gasped. 'I can't tell one kid from another, not when they're that age!'

Angus threw him back into the snow like a discarded sack.

'Poor Angus,' Elizabeth said. 'I'm so sorry.'

He looked up in the gloom and saw the pale oval of her face. She was shivering. He felt a compassion for her. The tension and long hard ride of the night, and the cold, were taking a toll on her slight young body. He rubbed her hands to get the blood flowing.

'We best get you home,' he said. 'Your folks will be worried sick.'

'No they won't,' she responded quickly. 'They won't be worried at all.'

'Why not?'

'Because I told them I'd be with you, Angus.'

Had he been in better spirits, he would have felt flattered. As it was, he pondered for a moment. 'Well, we'll ride for Kelly's Hole,' he said. 'We should be able to get some shelter there. Find somewhere warm and start back in the morning.'

'Yes, Angus.'

The old man, still tied on the ground, was struggling to sit up. 'Don't tell Johnny I tripped your horse up,' he pleaded. 'He'd kill me if he knew I'd done that to a horse.'

Angus grunted. He felt the old man was not quite right mentally.

He slipped his foot into the stirrup,

pulled himself into the saddle, and as he and Elizabeth edged their horses up the slope, he took a quick backward glance. Arabella had rushed out from the cabin to her prostrated husband, her young tongue berating him like that of an experienced shrew.

★   ★   ★

Kelly's Hole was a dead-bit place at the best of times, just a collection of shacks and small buildings, some of sod, some of logs, cast haphazardly on the prairie like buffalo droppings. In the small hours of a dreary night, with the snow thickening, a person couldn't have wished for a less cosy place. The settlement had originally been erected in a dip resembling a huge buffalo-wallow. This had been fine for protection against the sharp prairie winds, but come storms and rain the place became flooded.

As they rode up what purported to be main street, Angus spotted a sign swinging in the wind: KELLY'S GRAND GUEST HOUSE. Their horses needed little encouragement to trail to a halt. Angus slid from his saddle and banged his fist against the door. They waited an age, then a lantern flared from within and the door was opened by a scrawny man in a striped nightshirt.

With ill-grace, he agreed to provide shelter for both travellers and horses, though what crazy reasons they had for being abroad on such a foul night he could not imagine. The place was ramshackle and grubby, but after the discomforts of the outside world, it provided welcome shelter.

Their host poked some life into an open fire, put on two big logs, and supplied blankets for his guests. Angus said they would sit by the fire until the morning. The man nodded and shuffled off to his bed.

Without emotion Angus helped Elizabeth remove her wet outer garments, and suddenly it came to him that she was not a child, but a woman with fine young breasts. She was drawing her soft body against his, and there was a trembling in her, an intensity that frightened him.

'Oh, Angus,' she murmured huskily.

'You mustn't catch a cold,' he said, and swiftly drew a blanket about her.

He did the same for himself, and they sat by the fire. He knew she was annoyed with him. Presently he heard her breathing become steady and she rested on his shoulder. She had drifted into sleep. For a long time he listened to the wind ravaging outside, the draught down the chimney having the flames in the fireplace dancing, and in those flames he swore he saw Leah's face.

The disappointment of not finding Anna rested inside him like a heavy stone, but eventually sheer weariness drew him into slumber.

When the first glimmer of morning light showed through the windows, thinning the shadows in the room, he was awake. An idea was in his mind, like a chick struggling to escape the egg. It represented a remote possibility. Perhaps all was not lost.

★　★　★

Run down though the guest-house was, the owner certainly laid on a hearty breakfast of eggs, pork, flapjacks and strong black coffee. As Angus and Elizabeth sat at the saw-horse table, Angus posed a question to their host.

'Is there a doctor in Kelly's Hole?'

'Are you crazy!' The other man looked at him as if he was out of his head. 'You'll have to ride twenty miles to see a doctor.'

Angus nodded, frowning. 'How do they go for birthing here, then? Is there a midwife?'

'Why . . . is this young lady expectin'? She sure looks mighty slim.'

Elizabeth blushed, shaking her head.

'No, it's not that,' Angus said. 'It's just something I need to ask.'

The host looked totally mystified. 'Bertha Hopkins,' he said. 'End of street, left hand side. She ain't exactly over-employed here.'

Angus said: 'Thanks,' and tucked into his breakfast while his mind pondered.

A half-hour later he and Elizabeth struggled through the snow to the end of the street, passing a dozen or so dilapidated dwellings and a store. At least the wind had eased now. They found the home of Mrs Bertha Hopkins and knocked on her door. She opened up, a questioning expression on her round face. She was a big and strong woman with wispy grey hair.

Angus gave her his warmest smile and, overcoming her initial reluctance to divulge details of her recent work, he eventually gained the information he sought. Yes, two little ladies had taken up abode in the district during the past couple of years. One of them had died in her mother's arms. The other belonged to the Bevan family a half-mile down the trail from Kelly's

Hole — a strange couple, according to Bertha Hopkins.

Soon, Angus and Elizabeth had recovered their horses from their overnight stable and had ridden down the trail to where the Bevans lived in their small-holding. A burly man in a yellow slicker was brooming snow away from his cabin door. He paused when he saw the approaching riders and looked up, his face inhospitable.

'You got a young child here?' Angus enquired.

'What the hell is it to you?' Bevan responded, gripping his broom as if it were a weapon.

'I'm from Linus Kypp,' Angus said, then he played his hunch. 'He . . . he sent us over to collect the child.'

Mention of the Kypp name seemed to do some sort of trick. Bevan's attitude softened. 'Where's our kid, then? She all right?'

'Ay, she's fine,' Angus nodded.

Bevan looked somewhat uncertain. 'Trouble over, then?' he asked.

'Everything's OK.' Angus dismounted. He glanced up at Elizabeth. She was looking pale and drawn, holding her breath in suspense.

At last Bevan nodded towards the cabin door. Angus pushed it open and walked through, immediately meeting the puzzled gaze of a deprived looking woman.

'Linus sent the money, like he said?' she wanted to know.

'Later,' Angus said, but his mind wasn't on his speech.

In the corner of the room was a baby's cot.

He rushed over and peered into it, and the name rose to his lips of its own accord. 'Anna!'

16

Within half-an-hour they were embarked upon the long ride home. Angus, riding ahead, kept glancing over his shoulder at Elizabeth and the blanket-wrapped Anna she held. He had to keep looking to convince himself he was not dreaming. To him, having his daughter back, his and Leah's little girl, was more wondrous than anything else in the world. It was like having part of Leah back.

As they travelled he drew together his interpretation of events. Clearly Glaswall had sheltered at the Kypp place after his release from prison, but he and Johnny seemed to have fallen out over something — and old man Kypp had taken Glaswall's side, turning Johnny out. Only after Arabella's nagging did Linus Kypp ride to Pawnee Bend and make reconciliation with his son.

Glaswall had obviously formed some sort of relationship with Arabella and promised he'd get a baby to make up for the offspring Linus could not give her. Glaswall had raped Leah, kidnapped little Anna and handed her over to Arabella Kypp, who'd made her husband promise never to divulge the secret. When Angus had somehow extracted the clue as to his daughter's whereabouts, old Linus had ridden hard for his home, getting well ahead of Angus. He'd then sent Arabella to swap babies with their neighbours, the Bevans, promising them, no doubt, a good recompense. To make doubly sure of forestalling Angus, he'd ambushed him, maybe would have killed him had not Elizabeth intervened. Even with the ambush failing, he must have figured that when Angus found a different baby at the Kypp homestead, he would return home.

But things had not worked out that way.

As they eventually neared Pawnee

Bend, Angus's euphoria was levelling out. So overwhelmed had he been at rescuing his daughter that he had given no thought as to how he would look after her. Without his beloved Leah, how would he cope?

* * *

It was afternoon when they reached town. Elizabeth rushed away, taking Anna with her, while Angus took the horses to the livery. Afterwards he walked to the Claytons' house. As he stepped inside, a shock awaited him.

Johnny Kypp was sitting in the surgery, while Edmund Clayton fixed a sling for his arm.

'Johnny was lucky that the bullet just burned a groove in his shoulder,' the doctor said, then he gave Angus a smile. 'Wonderful news about finding your babe!'

Angus heartily agreed, but now he found himself meeting the cold eyes of Johnny Kypp and the old hate was rising in him.

For a moment he was speechless. Then he broke the uneasy silence.

'That's your right shoulder you've hurt, Johnny,' he said. 'Seems you won't be able to handle a gun for a while.'

'I can use my left hand,' Johnny said.

'But you won't be so fast, eh?'

Johnny ran his tongue across his lips. 'That's why I wanted to see you, Angus Troon.'

'I would've thought you'd want to keep out of my way,' Angus said sourly.

Johnny shook his head. 'I got news today. A telegram came through. It said that Duquemain has escaped from the penitentiary!'

A cold sickness struck Angus.

'And one thing's sure as Texas,' Johnny went on. 'He sure ain't no friend of yours.'

Angus tried to steady his breathing. He'd always dreaded the day Duquemain would be free of jail, knowing full well that the outlaw would make a beeline for him and there would be a gun in his hand.

'Before me and Glaswall were let loose,' Johnny said, 'Duquemain came up to us in the exercise yard. He went over how it was you who got us shut away. How he was gonna get his own back, come hell or high water. He made us promise that we would make life hell for you, but not to kill you. He wanted that pleasure for hisself.'

Angus tried to shut out from his ears what he was hearing, but the words seemed to echo inside his head.

'How long since he escaped?' he asked.

'A week ago.'

'Why are you warning me, Johnny Kypp?'

Kypp spoke slowly, as if it was great strain on him. 'Because I need your help. Duquemain hates your guts like poison. He also hates mine. He'll want me dead, almost as much as he does you.'

'Why does he hate you?' Angus said.

'I thought you were his buddy.'

'He hates me because I broke my promise to him. The only way I harmed you was to trash your vegetable patch. When Glaswall talked about killin' your horses, I refused to play a part. Glaswall murdered them horses, lovely animals, and I've never forgiven him. I've had nothin' to do with the other things that've happened to you. That was all Glaswall, and I ain't seen him since. Now, I hear, he and Duquemain are sayin' I betrayed them, and they swear I'll die alongside you.'

'My God!' Edmund Clayton exclaimed. His thin face had drained of colour. He was as stunned as Angus.

Angus was striving to make sense of Johnny's revelations. If they were true, he realized that he had little to hold against the younger Kypp — apart from him having the most ornery father this side of Christendom.

'So you expect me to help you against Duquemain and Glaswall?' Angus asked, striving to keep the incredulity out of his voice.

'I'm askin' you to be my deputy — fully paid deputy town marshal.'

Angus's jaw dropped somewhat. 'That's crazy!'

'But true,' Johnny Kypp confirmed.

* * *

Next day, Sunday, was bright and cold. After church, Angus walked up to the cemetery on the edge of town. Moving amid the headstones he soon located Leah's grave. He placed the dainty pot of cyclamens he had brought at the base of the headstone. Then he knelt on the ground and in his mind communicated with the woman he had loved so dearly, the image of her happy face, her smile, filling his thoughts. He recalled the time before their marriage, when they had wandered through the summer flowers hand in hand and he smiled. He knew Leah would be overjoyed, wherever she was, that little Anna was safe and well.

But he realized that he must do right by his daughter. It was unfair to rely on the good-heartedness of Elizabeth Clayton and her mother for much longer. He owed the family a great deal. They were God-fearing folks of the highest order.

At that moment he heard somebody coming through the cemetery gate behind him. He turned and Elizabeth stood close by, as if conjured from his thoughts by magic into reality. For a second his eyes lingered on her pale face, seeing the gentleness, the soft warmth of nature that was so much part of her. She was reserved and yet she had shown considerable resolution when she had forced Linus Kypp to submit. Within her, Angus knew, she had immense courage for one who was scarcely more than a child.

She stepped forward and placed a small posy of wild heather alongside his cyclamens, then she turned towards him with almost a challenge in her blue eyes.

'Angus,' she said, 'I know it's been preying on your mind — about Anna I mean.'

'Ay,' he nodded. 'I can't rely on you and your ma for ever. You've been so kind to me, but I have to find somewhere permanent for her. I've got a cousin in the East. She has four children of her own. I'll write to her and ask her if she will bring Anna up. She's a good soul.'

Elizabeth's eyes hardened. 'Oh Angus, you'll do no such thing. Mother and I have discussed it. We'd love to care for Anna on a permanent basis, and she would be close to you.'

Angus saw it then: the same female possessiveness that he'd seen blazing from Arabella's eyes when he'd taken his child away from her. He understood now the challenge that Elizabeth had displayed when she'd first approached him. She'd feared that he might refuse her offer.

Uncertain, he gazed at Leah's grave, in the hope that his wife might offer him some guidance. Then he turned back.

'I appreciate your kindness, Elizabeth, but I need to think it over,' he said. 'Of course I would have to discuss it with your mother. I don't think it would be fair.'

Despair spread across the girl's face. 'Please, Angus. It's not just for your sake, not just for Anna's sake. We love her. We'd be heartbroken if we had to give her up, really heartbroken.'

He reached across and took her arm and they walked through the cemetery gate. She seemed so small alongside him.

'I'll let you know tomorrow,' he said.

17

Angus felt that one difficult decision per day was quite sufficient. Today he must sort matters out with Johnny Kypp. The mere proximity of the man aroused hostility and suspicion inside him. But circumstances beyond his control had placed him in the craziest of situations. A stark choice had to be made. He must either trust Kypp — or kill him!

When he stepped into the marshal's office, he found Kypp sitting at the desk, thumbing through some papers, the marshal's badge pinned to his vest. His pistol was unholstered on the desk before him, and now he looked up, his eyes widening to take in Angus as he loomed over him.

'You offered me the job of deputy,' Angus said. 'I want to hear your version of events before I say yes or no.'

Kypp pursed his lips, eyeing him coldly.

'I don't care about how you got involved with the bank robbery,' Angus went on. 'You paid the penalty. That's in the past. It's what happened after you came out of prison, I want to know about, and why my wife was murdered!' He choked on the last words. They sounded so stark.

Kypp said, 'You'd better sit down, Angus Troon. Ain't no point in standing there like a thunder-cloud.'

Angus lowered himself on to a chair. He was reluctant to lower his guard when near this man, but he must give him his chance to speak. Maybe, just maybe, he had misjudged him. At any rate, there was a lot of explaining to do.

Kypp took a deep breath as if bracing himself for what he had to say. He rested his hands on the desk before him, inches from his gun.

'Like I told you,' he began, 'I got mixed up with the wrong crowd. Robbin' the bank was bad. I should never have got involved, but I sure paid the penalty, and I have no intention of gettin' put back behind bars.'

He paused, seeming to compose his thoughts. This was a new side of Johnny Kypp, but Angus was still suspicious.

'I can tell you,' Kypp went on, 'Duquemain's as mean as sin. They don't come no meaner. He made me and Glaswall swear to make your life hell, until he could get at you himself. And now he's on the loose, so you'd better keep your wits about you, Angus Troon. And so had I, 'cos he sure hates me for goin' back on my word. All I did was trash your vegetables, after that I didn't have any truck with what Glaswall had in mind, killin' them horses and all. The whole thing sickened me.'

'My wife's dead!' Angus exploded. 'My life has been ruined!'

'I never had anythin' to do with that. I agree, it's terrible, should never have happened. I never dreamed Glaswall would go that far.'

Angus felt his emotions boiling. 'So it was Glaswall who did that to Leah.'

Kypp nodded solemnly. 'I used to think he had some humanity in his soul, but I was wrong. Trouble is, Arabella was broody and desperate. The old man couldn't give her what she wanted — a kid of her own. So Glaswall promised he'd get her a baby — and she was happy enough, until you turned up.'

Angus raised an accusing finger towards Kypp. 'But you knew that what was goin' on was the blackest of sins.'

'Not until after it happened, and that's God's truth. If I'd known, I'd have found some way of stoppin' Glaswall.'

'How come your old man got himself such a young wife?' Angus asked.

'Oh . . . Arabella. She married Dad for his money, I guess. He's got quite a bit salted away. I won't tell you how he came by it. But she got more than she bargained for — not just money.'

Angus nodded, not knowing whether to believe this man or not.

201

Kypp raised his hands, palms towards Angus as if in a sign of peace. 'Look, you and I've gotta trust each other. Duquemain and Glaswall want us both dead, and I can tell you, it's either us or them. They're gonna show up in these parts mighty soon, that's for sure. I've got this injured shoulder which don't help none. But I reckon that together we'll stand a better chance. Take on the job of deputy, Angus Troon.'

Conflicting thoughts battled in Angus's brain. 'How do I know I can trust you?' he asked.

'You can,' Kypp said emphatically. 'I give you my word. Let's shake on it.'

With some effort, because his shoulder pained him, he extended his injured right hand. 'You take the job of deputy. Let's shake on it.'

Angus gazed at the hand of the man he had hated for so long, the hand that hung there like a leaf waiting to fall. Kypp had formed the very core of his hatred for months. It wasn't easy to adjust his mind, yet if the story he'd told was true, what he was suggesting made sense. Angus gazed into Kypp's brooding eyes, trying to find something that would prove the man was being honest. He found nothing but, tentatively, he reached out, their hands touched and then grasped each other in a shake.

'We'll go across and see the mayor,' Kypp said, 'and get you sworn in as paid deputy town marshal.'

★　★　★

Johnny Kypp seemed to have his office well organized. He worked out a roster for duties in which he and Angus took turns. These included hours at manning the desk, patrols around town, keeping an eye on the saloon and generally scouting for trouble. There was also the young, part-time deputy Dave Sangster. The last time Angus had seen him was when he had been crawling out from beneath Squirrel-Tooth Sally.

With things running pretty quiet in town, the demands of the job were not great. Angus found himself with alternate days free, and spent as much time as he could with baby Anna, who was pink and beautiful and gurgling with happiness. He made her a wooden rocking-horse and her laughter was a joy to hear.

He didn't see much of Johnny Kypp, except when they handed over duties. He wondered if he was spending his spare time at the family homestead. Kypp's right arm had stiffened from the wound he'd taken, and he took to wearing his gun on the left side and practising with his left hand. Neither man was over-talkative by nature, and Angus was content to keep it that way. He had the feeling that events would unfurl very soon.

Old suspicions lingered with him, along with the knowledge that Duquemain and Glaswall were at large and dangerous. Angus would welcome the appearance of both men, particularly

Glaswall. Each passing day strengthened his belief in what Johnny Kypp
had told him, strengthened his hatred
for the man who had brought about the
death of his beloved wife. And he would
know no peace until Glaswall had paid
for his dreadful sin.

One night he dreamed that he had
suddenly met Glaswall and Duquemain
face to face in the street. And he
emptied his gun into them and enjoyed
a moment of nigh orgasmic exaltation
as the two men sprawled at his feet,
bleeding and dying. The dream was so
strong, so vivid, that he experienced
great disappointment when he awoke to
reality.

On Saturday morning, a number of
reward posters arrived on the morning
stage and were delivered to the office.
The Kansas Territorial Legislature had
offered a reward of $5000 for the
capture, dead or alive, of Duquemain.
Angus ensured that the posters were
displayed around town.

Then, the following afternoon, events

took a surprising turn. Elizabeth rushed to the office through the snow, nigh slipping over in her haste. She handed Angus a letter.

'Ivan Polanski delivered this,' she panted. 'He asked me to give it to you.'

Angus felt puzzled. Polanski and his family were Russian immigrants and they ran a farm a half-mile east from Troon's Ferry, now renamed Kruger's Ferry. He tore open the letter, not recognizing the scrawled handwriting on the note.

Angus Troon
I have important news for you. I'm staying with the Polanski family. I have run away from the Kypps. Terrible things have happened. I must see you. You are in great danger. Come to the Polanski place tomorrow evening. I will tell you everything. Burn this immediately. If Johnny sees it, I am dead!
Your friend
Arabella Kypp

'What is it?' Elizabeth asked.

Angus had implicit trust in the girl. He passed her the note to read. He produced matches from his pocket and tore one off from the block. When Elizabeth returned the paper, he set light to it and burned it to ashes.

'You won't go, will you?' Elizabeth said anxiously. 'It's probably a trap.'

Angus pondered for a moment, then shook his heart. 'It might be,' he conceded. 'On the other hand, it might not. There's only one way to find out.'

'Oh God, Angus,' she gasped, her grey eyes full of concern. 'You'll have to be so careful.'

He recalled when another person had murmured a similar warning to him.

18

He left in the morning of next day. As he rode a great owl swooped so low that Angus felt the stir of air from the slow beat of its silent wings. He was hunched in his buckskin coat. It was bitterly cold, the wind gusting snow in his face, and Judas slipped more than once. He wondered whether he was being lured into a trap. Were Duquemain and Glaswall awaiting him at the Polanski farm? He figured that giving himself plenty of time before his evening appointment would allow him to keep watch on the farm during the afternoon to see if anything aroused his suspicions. If either of the outlaws showed himself, he would shoot at him, and with the prospect of bullets flying, he had been insistent that Elizabeth should remain behind. She'd already risked so much for him.

He turned off the trail a half-mile before it reached the ferry. He struck east, and well before noon he was hidden up in the aspens overlooking the Polanski farm, where smoke rose from a chimney. There was an orderliness about it that was typical of the Russian immigrants, with neat fences and well organized barns for storing wheat.

He watched the place through his eye-glass during the long, icy hours of the afternoon. He saw both Ivan Polanski and his wife Olga step out, well wrapped up, to use the outhouse. Ivan worked for an hour or so in the barn, then went back to the house. As the light faded lights showed from the windows. If Arabella was down there, or any of the outlaws, they were keeping well hidden. The thought occurred to Angus that Arabella might be so bitter about his removing Anna that she herself might be planning some vengeance. On any account, he knew that he must be vigilant.

Now, with night deepening, he

decided it was time for action. He tethered Judas back in the aspens and descended until he reached the open slope. Beneath him light from the farmhouse glowed through the curtained windows. He paused to check that his gun was ready, then he cupped his hands to his mouth and unleashed a loud 'Hi there!'

There was no response, so he repeated the call.

This time he heard the rattle of bolts being drawn back on the main door, and it opened to allow light to spew across the porch. In the doorway a bulky figure was silhouetted — Ivan Polanski.

'Who is there?' the farmer called in his thick Russian accent.

Angus felt disinclined to shout his name into the night.

'You left a note,' he shouted. 'I've come to see Arabella Kypp.'

The man visibly relaxed. 'Welcome,' he called. 'Come in.'

Angus paced forward, well aware that

his shadowy figure would be an easy target against the snowy back-ground of the slope. His eyes darting around him, his nerves on edge and his hand resting on the butt of his gun, he made the descent. He was ready to plunge to the side at the first hint of danger, but none came, and a moment later he found himself stepping up on to the porch.

The Russian faced him, his hand extended in greeting.

'Come along inside, my friend,' he said. 'It is too cold out here. Arabella is waiting. She has had a terrible ordeal.'

Angus shook the man's hand, feeling he was sincere. He entered the main room of the house, where a big fire blazed in a stone fireplace and the fresh-cut logs filled the air with crackle. Angus was surprised by the numerous icons of sacred personages and egg-shaped, lacquered miniatures that adorned the walls, and the dozens of clay figurines in a glass-fronted cabinet. But he had little inclination to admire them.

The two women were seated at the table, turning to look at him.

'Meet my wife, Olga,' Polanski said, indicating the woman in a loose-fitting dress. 'I think you already know Arabella. She has taken shelter with us.'

Angus nodded a greeting to Olga, then his attention swung to Arabella and he grunted with shock. The left side of her face was black and swollen with bruises, and there was an ugly cut which only just missed her eye.

'What's happened?' he gasped.

'I run away from the Kypps,' Arabella cried. 'I never want see them again. My husband . . . he do this.'

She pointed a trembling finger at the brutal marks on her face.

'He say I nag him; he say he cannot stand my tongue any more. But I never nagged. I only say what is right.' She paused to take in a shuddering breath. 'But Johnny is worst. He knock me down, rip me naked and . . . '

'Johnny?' Angus said.

'*Sí* . . . It was him. He rape me!' Her lips were quivering, her eyes spilling with tears. 'And my husband, he stand and watch and . . . he laugh!'

Angus gasped.

'And you know what Johnny say?' the Mexican girl went on. 'He say: *that hoity-toity Troon woman enjoy it. Why shouldn't you!*'

'No!' Angus recoiled with horror.

Olga Polanski placed a comforting arm around the girl's shoulders and voiced soothing words in Russian.

Angus felt utterly sick. He wanted to block out from his ears, from his senses, what he had heard.

He gazed at his hand in disgust. He had touched Johnny Kypp's hand. If what Arabella had said was true, he had shaken the hand that had violated Leah. Angry bile rose in his throat and he swallowed it back.

As Arabella was drying her eyes with the handkerchief that Olga had given her, he struggled to control his pounding emotions. 'And my wee lass,

213

Anna?' he gasped. 'Was it Johnny who stole her?'

Arabella nodded. 'It was him, but he say to claim Glaswall did it. If Johnny or my husband knew I was here they would find me and kill me. Johnny is as bad as Glaswall doing those awful things to you. They are both evil as the devil and so is Linus! He say if I run away, he find me, drag me back!'

She lapsed into a hysterical bout of sobbing.

Ivan Polanski rested his hand on Angus's shoulder. 'It has been a shock for you, my friend. I will get you some whiskey — or perhaps vodka?'

Angus's chest was heaving with wrath. 'No, I can't stop. I must find Johnny Kypp.'

'You no tell Johnny I . . . ' Arabella cried out in alarm.

Angus cut across her. 'I won't breathe a word about you.'

★   ★   ★

Struggling angrily through the snow, Angus returned to Judas and untethered him. A moment later he was heeling him along the forest trail. He had no real way of telling whom to believe. Anybody could have inflicted those bruises on Arabella. The fact was that she was seething with hatred for Johnny, and such blistering hatred had not been previously evident.

Perhaps the real answer was that all three, Johnny Kypp, Duquemain and Glaswall, should stand trial before a proper judge and be hanged! But if the opportunity arose to kill them himself Angus knew what he would do. The time to ask questions would be after they were in their graves.

At first he was too preoccupied with his own thoughts to notice how the low night-clouds were reflecting a redness above the trees. It was only as he passed close to his old home, the ferry house, that he realized that the redness was caused by flames, and now the acrid smell of smoke tainted the night air. He turned Judas towards the house, along trails which were as familiar as the back of his hand.

Ten minutes later, he reined in and gasped with shock. The entire house was a crackling blaze, flames and sparks rearing high into the sky like furious red serpents, being drawn into an awesome vortex by the buffeting wind. He saw several figures dashing here and there, silhouetted against the blazing house. He recognized the Teutonic shouting of Otto Kruger mingling with the roar of cracking timbers. To one side of the house, safely back, he saw the Kruger family standing, the girls in their night clothes, clutching their dolls, watching their home disintegrate in the blazing inferno.

Angus heeled his reluctant sorrel forward. He wondered whether he might be able to provide assistance. Kruger was leading his panicking horses away from the fire, striving to calm them, his anguished features illuminated by the flames. He'd released his hogs, and they were scuttling about, desperate to escape the heat. He spotted Angus approaching and turned towards him.

'You'll pay for this, Angus Troon,' he yelled, his cheeks puffed out with anger. 'I won't let it rest!'

Angus reined in alongside the German. 'Pay . . . what do you mean?'

'They are your enemies, not mine!' Kruger cried, his bullish face shining with sweat. 'They did this because they hated you.'

'Who?' gasped Angus.

'They shouted out your name and started shooting at the windows, then they threw flaming torches onto the roof. One of them was shouting in French. There was nothing we could do, except hope they didn't kill us as we rushed out, damn their souls to hell! They were after you, not me. You should have told me about the danger before you took my money, my life savings.'

Angus cursed. Clearly this was the

work of Duquemain and most likely Glaswall. They must have believed that Angus still owned the ferry.

'I'll help you,' Angus said.

'*Ja*! You can help me. Get off my land! You'll pay for this, or I'll see you dead!'

'Where are the two men now?' Angus demanded.

Kruger waved his hand vaguely up-river, and then stamped away, leading his horses across the snow. Angus hesitated, then he shouted: 'I'll get after them.'

He heeled Judas in the direction that Kruger had indicated, anger dulling any thought of fatigue.

19

'Troon!' The shout was barely discernible above the pound of Judas's hoofs, the crackle of burning timbers and the bluster of wind. A few yards more, and Angus would have been unaware of it.

'Troon!' It pierced the night, stabbing at him like a knife in the back as he followed along the north bank of the Peigan. Reluctantly, he hauled on Judas's reins, dragging him to a halt. He turned, gazed back along the way he had come.

A single horseman was approaching rapidly, waving his arm. It was Otto Kruger. He was gesticulating wildly as he drew close.

'Troon,' he shouted. 'Hold on!'

Irritation flooded through Angus. Had the German decided to inflict retribution on him immediately, instead of waiting for a later moment?

Kruger halted his mount alongside Angus, the panted words tumbling out of him. 'Like I said, you will pay for what has happened, but firstly, those swine have got to be tracked down, brought to justice. It is best we work together. Two guns are better than one.'

'But how about your family? You can't just leave them in the cold.'

Kruger brushed aside the objection. 'Hanna is well able to drive a wagon. She will take the children to Pawnee Bend. We have friends there. Now let us get on. We must catch them, shoot them down before they do more harm!'

'Ay,' Angus said. 'We'll ride together. I figure they might have followed the river northward beyond the rapids. They won't be able to cross over. They'll probably make for the high country. We may be following the wrong trail, but I don't think so. One thing's sure. They won't want to linger around here for long.'

Kruger grunted his agreement.

'Let's ride then! Let's catch the swine!'

They slammed their heels into the flanks of their animals and they were away.

Fifteen minutes later, the glimmer of a camp-fire showed in the trees on their left. Both riders halted their animals, then Angus led the way cautiously forward. Soon the aroma of coffee came to them on the icy air. Closer in, they saw a small canvas-topped wagon drawn up, a horse wearing a nosebag close by. A man and a woman were huddled near the fire, over which a kettle hung on a tripod. The man was feeding wood into the flames.

'Hullo there!' Angus called from the concealment of the trees. 'We mean you no harm.'

Both man and woman were on their feet instantly, their faces registering alarm. A gun had suddenly appeared in the man's hands. But Angus called again calmingly 'I'm Deputy Marshal of Pawnee Bend. We're chasing after outlaws. Two men.'

As Angus and Kruger revealed themselves, the couple relaxed.

'There's coffee if you want it,' the man said, his voice Russian. They were clearly immigrants, no doubt heading towards their fellows, intent on settling.

Angus nodded his thanks but said: 'We haven't time for coffee. Have any riders passed this way?'

It was the woman who answered.

'*Da*! They didn't stop. Two men riding fast, following the river. I do not think they saw us. We hadn't lit the fire then.'

Angus nodded with satisfaction. 'We must push on.'

They bade farewell to the Russian couple and forced their way through the night, following the river, seeing the dark hulk of the high country rising before them against the snow-heavy sky. A crazy thought probed at Angus. He recalled how he'd ventured this way before, and chance had drawn him to the deserted campsite at the top of an abyss. It was certainly a point that afforded an unrivalled view of the surrounding country and everything that moved in it. Was it possible that it was towards this that the two outlaws were now headed? He tried to dismiss the thought. It was too much of a coincidence. Fate had never been that kind to him! And yet, as they rode on, the idea persisted. And when they reached a point where the trail branched upward, away from the river and towards the soaring terrain, Judas turned that way, as if drawn by instinct.

They paused every half-hour or so to rest their flagging mounts. The going was hard through the snow. Judas was particularly weary after the long miles he had been ridden. Kruger remained uncommunicative, still apparently harbouring resentment against Angus and blaming him for all his troubles. But he seemed content enough to follow along and Angus did not hanker for conversation; he was too busy trying to align his thoughts with those of their enemies.

But all the reasoning he could muster did not save him from disaster.

The formal trail, almost indistinguishable beneath the snow, had long since petered out, giving way to boulder-strewn, treacherous slope. With the the dreary grey of dawn now upon them, Angus had overlooked the possibility that instead of being the hunters, Kruger and himself might find themselves the prey.

They entered a narrow upward-slanting ravine, shielded from the immediate fall of snow — a groove through the rock carved by some primeval upheaval. They were enclosed by overhanging walls of ice-cloaked stone. Angus was briefly aware of the chattering of Kruger's teeth.

They had entered the perfect trap — as Duquemain and Glaswall, who had been aware of pursuit for some time, well knew. Guns drawn, they were ready and waiting.

The crack of gunfire created an awesome, echoing whiplash of sound within the narrow confines of the ravine.

Both horses were struck. Judas dropped to his knees and Angus was jerked from his saddle, plunging over the sorrel's head, stunned by the swiftness of the attack. He lost track of Kruger's fate. After a crunching fall, he rolled over in the snow, then his skull cracked against something hard and he lost consciousness.

He was unaware of Henri Duquemain and Silas Glaswall clambering down from their hiding-place to stand triumphantly over their fallen pursuers, slipping their heated pistols back into their leather.

The dark, silver-bearded features of Duquemain showed great concern as he stooped over Angus's prostrate body. But as he leaned close and confirmed that the ferryman's chest still rose and fell, he grunted with satisfaction. It was not part of his plan that Angus Troon should expire right now. That would be too easy for him. Duquemain had a far more gruesome fate in mind for this man — a fate far more fitting to avenge the wrong he considered the ferryman had done him.

'Let us get zem up to ze camp,' he said to Glaswall.

Glaswall nodded. 'Reckon we'll tie 'em up first. Don't want them havin' no fancy ideas of runnin' off.'

★ ★ ★

When Angus groaned his way back to sensibility a paroxysm of pain nearly caused him to faint. He considered that his pain was too intense to bear, that, like a newborn baby striving to return to the womb, all he wished for was to lapse back into the bliss of his previous oblivion. But such mercy was not forthcoming. It seemed only death would bring respite.

Gritting his teeth, he struggled to move his limbs but found his efforts severely thwarted. His hands were fastened behind his back. He tried to reason out the exact nature of his predicament and could not.

He was sitting in an extremely cramped position. His chin was thrust hard against his knees. His head was forced to one side by the low roof above and, had he wished to turn his shoulders, he was so constricted that it would have been impossible. He felt as if he was in a tiny, sit-up coffin, more suitable for a dwarf than a six-foot man. Through narrow cracks he could see that daylight had come — but, beyond the narrowest gleam of light, he was unable to distinguish any other feature of the outside world.

His teeth were chattering with the cold.

Then he became aware of the outside wind gusting, and at the same time he felt the contraption that imprisoned him swaying back and forth. Suddenly the awesome truth exploded in his mind — a lightning flash revealing his darkest terrors.

That day when he was searching the

mountains he'd crawled to the very brink of the soaring bluff. With his insides quaking, he'd gazed down into the vertiginous depths and been plagued by his compulsive fear of heights. Later, he'd examined the Osage contrivance for protecting meat from wild depredation — by dangling it by rope in the crate, suspended down the cliff-face.

He shuddered.

At the time he'd considered the crate big enough to take a man — just. Now he realized he'd been right!

In desperation he moved his head, forcing it against the side of his prison in an attempt to do the work that his bound arms could not. His effort was futile. Beneath him were dizzy depths, separated from him only by thin boarding fashioned by long-gone Indian hands; his life dependent upon meagre strands of rope which bore the weight of man and crate.

Panic lifted inside him like a suffocating, red sea and he screamed out.

It was then, as he lapsed back, panting like a dog, aware of cold sweat streaming over his face, that he heard the sound of scornful laughter from above him, and a voice, heavy with French accent, taunted him.

'*Mon bon ami*, Angus Troon, I zink you wish you didn't open your mouth in zat courtroom, eh? But you must suffer now. I 'ave my knife 'ere. I must say *au revoir*, and cut the rope. I 'ope you 'ave a pleasant trip and enjoy the 'eavy landing — ha!'

Angus felt a severe rocking of the crate. He grew rigid with dread. He guessed the knife was slicing into the unresisting rope. Once it was severed he would be plummeting downward . . . downward.

It no longer seemed relevant, but he discovered a slight looseness in the rope linking his wrists. He strained against it, working on it frantically.

20

Old Linus Kypp lashed his decrepit mare angrily up the snow-slippery slope, cursing that she could not eat up the miles like she used to. Mind you, the going was tough as he circled a drift and passed through the tangle of aspen and spruce, the cold making the knife-scars on his cheeks stand out, while the brush clawed at his stumpy legs and left red streaks along the lathered flanks of the horse.

Linus had made a promise to himself. He was not going to let any two-timing female, especially one no more than a third of his age, make a fool of him. He had given Arabella the respectability of the Kypp name, provided her with a marital home and bed. He had even knuckled down to her constant tongue-lashing. She had repaid him by playing up to another man, and afterwards had run off, no doubt trailing after yet another fellow, meanwhile flashing her favours to all and sundry.

Of course at first he had figured that the affair with Johnny had been just a bit of fun, high youthful spirits and nothing more to it. But later he saw things differently. She'd had no compunction about cheating on her husband and benefactor. So he'd shown her that, although he was small in stature, he was still capable of whipping a female into shape. Nothing more than a few bruises and cuts, mind. He'd never guessed she'd go and commit the most grievous sin that any legally married woman can — run off.

Now it was pay-back time.

So Linus Kypp had trailed after her, determined to give her a another good whipping, then drag her back home and make sure she behaved herself. He'd hunted high and low, finding no sign, and almost figured he might have to go to Mexico to find her. Then an idea had come upon him. He'd reasoned that maybe Glaswall was the target of her lust. And knowing that Duquemain was at large once more, he'd recalled their old hideout — the cliff-top camp, once the haunt of the Osage Indians. He had in fact recommended the place to Johnny over eight years ago as a good hideaway if the law was after you. Johnny had, in turn, told Duquemain about it. Now it was, most likely, where the Frenchman was holed up, Glaswall with him and, God willing, Arabella too. Linus felt quite smug with himself at having reasoned it all out.

So here he was, breathing the thin air as he kicked the mare higher up the slope. Eventually he spotted a saddled, stocking-foot sorrel on the flat of a mountain meadow, muzzling into the snow for grass. The animal looked familiar, but he couldn't recall why. When he attempted to approach it it shifted off, not anxious to establish acquaintance. He noticed how its withers were glistening with blood. He debated whether he should put a bullet into the beast, but decided against it, as the sound of a shot would reveal his presence to unfriendly ears.

He rode on, the going becoming harder as the snow grew deeper, the breath of man and labouring beast clouding whitely. At last he topped out on the southern end of the great bluff. He figured he was about a mile from the camp and an old tingling in his water, an old excitement, barred any consideration that he might have got things wrong. Arabella would be there for sure, and if he had to kill Glaswall to get her back, so be it.

He leaned forward, unsheathed his mighty .50-calibre buffalo rifle from its scabbard, and satisfied himself that it was ready for when it was needed. He was thankful that he'd found his treasured weapon in the snow after he'd been tricked into dropping it by that slip of a girl who had a crush on Angus Troon.

Getting nearer, his keen nostrils

picked up a taint of smoke on the frigid air and he grunted with excitement. It took him another half-hour to circle around and approach the campsite through the tumble of boulders and low, thorny scrub.

He slipped from his saddle and left the mare standing head-dropped in the snow. What he had to do was best done on foot. He was surprisingly agile for his age, moving on his stumpy legs, sure-footed over the slippery rocks and wind-packed snow, like a goat. He smiled as he heard the clink of sound from the concealed campsite. This told him two things: firstly, there was somebody there; and secondly, they weren't expecting visitors.

The crest of the bluff was in the form of a curve; thus, before he reached it, he was afforded a view of the area in which the campsite was hidden. Glancing across the intervening void, he got a surprise. The old Indian crate, used for storing game, was dangling, like a giant spider on its thread, over the edge of the cliff, some fifteen feet down. And by the way it was jigging around, moving joltingly back and forth, it contained something heavy and very much alive, something that clearly objected to being imprisoned therein. Then, sounding quite clearly, he heard a scornful laugh, and his eyes, drawn to the sound, seized upon the man poised on the crest of the cliff. He was brandishing a *Georgius Rex* knife, making a big show as if about to cut the rope — and send the dangling crate crashing into the gorge.

The sight of the knife-wielding man, with his dark skin, stocky build, silver hair and beard brought another satisfied grunt to Linus Kypp's lips. He'd just *known* that Henri Duquemain would be here. But what was he up to, cutting that rope? And what, or who, was he planning to send plunging to certain death?

An image of Arabella's face jumped into Kypp's mind and he blasphemed. Maybe it was her in the crate. He felt sudden anger against Duquemain. If she needed to be punished, as surely she did, he would do it himself — and it wouldn't be in the form of sending her falling to a quick death in the depths.

He lifted his Sharps into his shoulder, recalling how there was a 'dead or alive' reward offered for Duquemain's head. He took careful aim, his gnarled finger tightening on the trigger. The Big Fifty's boom caused a flurry of wing-fluttering as alarmed birds rose in clouds from their cliff-face nests.

★ ★ ★

The *thock!* of the great buffalo gun came like an axe thudding into a tree; it had Otto Kruger opening his eyes, seeing how powder smoke had clouded up on the edge of the cliff that curved around on his right. He tried to move and could not. He was bound to a tree about twenty yards back from the abyss. He was in intense pain from the bullet that had entered his shoulder and he had lost a deal of blood. None

236

the less, he had been aware of events about him. He had watched, helpless to intervene, as the two outlaws had bundled the unconscious Angus Troon into the crate and tied its door firmly with rope. After this, they had lowered the laden contraption over the cliff edge.

The man called Glaswall had gone off to set some rabbit snares. Meanwhile, for maybe an hour, the dark-skinned Frenchman had had a great time taunting the entrapped Troon by pretending to cut the rope. No doubt he would eventually do so, but not before he'd driven his captive to distraction. Kruger had groaned, fearing that he might suffer the same fate, but then he took consolation in the fact that that would be impossible. The crate would no longer exist. It would be smashed to insignificant splinters on the rocks far below — and with it would be Angus Troon.

If the Frenchman had a grisly death in mind for Otto Kruger, it would have to be in a different form.

But now the sudden blast of the great buffalo gun had changed everything. The force of the bullet had struck Duquemain with such power that he had been flung forward headlong — and had vanished!

If his body was ever seen again, it would be in battered fragments on the rocks 200 feet below.

Kruger tried to wriggle free of his bonds, but failed. He felt light-headed and without strength. He was at the mercy of whoever had blasted Duquemain into eternity.

He was not kept waiting.

An old man, scarcely more than a dwarf, stomped from the trees, hastily ramming fresh cartridges into his Sharps.

At first Linus Kypp didn't see Kruger, secured as he was to a tree. It was only when the German groaned that the old man's eyes swung in that direction — and Kypp jumped with the shock of having overlooked such an obvious sight as a man fixed to a tree.

'Lookin' for my wife!' he shouted. 'Mexican girl. You seen her?'

The German, clearly feeling decidedly poorly, rolled his eyes. Then he gestured with his head, making an indication towards the brink of the cliff, the spot where the taut rope extended over the edge.

Linus Kypp immediately understood, remembering how that Indian meat-safe was dangling there.

'You mean she's . . . she's in that crate?'

Kruger seemed to nod.

A look of glee spread across Kypp's face. He glanced at the rope. He stepped across to it, gazed down at the top of crate suspended some fifteen feet below him. Whoever was inside had gone quiet.

'Don't worry, my pretty one,' he called down, cupping his hands to his thin lips. 'I'll soon haul you up.'

But as he tested the weighted rope, he knew it was beyond his strength. He cursed. 'You just wait there, Arabella. I'll get my horse to pull you up. I'll be back right soon.'

Kruger gazed at him with desperate eyes, hoping that the old man might release him before he disappeared, but Kypp scrambled off over the rocks, not sparing him a glance. Ten minutes later he was back, leading the weary mare.

Kypp worked with a feverish excitement, unfastening the rope from its rock-anchor and winding it around his saddle horn. He grunted with gratification as the old mare took up the strain, somehow establishing a footing on the slippery surface. He kicked her into moving away from the cliff edge. Yard by yard the dangling crate was hauled upward until its top was level with the crest. Striving to keep his footing, Kypp goaded the horse into a final effort and the wooden contrivance was dragged up over the brink on to the flat ground above. Kypp jumped forward, drawing his Bowie knife from the sheath on his belt. Swearing he would soon have his hands on his recalcitrant wife, he slashed through the cords fastening the door of the crate.

It was at that moment that Glaswall, drawn by the boom of the earlier shot, shouted as he appeared from the adjacent trees. 'Leave that crate alone, damn you!'

Linus Kypp swung around to face him, snarling like a rabid wolf. He lunged for his Sharps which he'd rested on the ground while he was manipulating the rope, momentarily thankful that he'd left it charged and ready — but his hand never grasped the weapon because Glaswall's bullet ploughed into his chest, hurling him backwards, slithering across the icy gradient and over the brink of the cliff. If he was conscious of his predicament, he made no sound as his dwarfish body plunged downward, growing smaller and smaller until eventually it was a disintegrated blob in the depths of the canyon.

Meanwhile, Angus had thrust open the door of the old crate, erupting out of it like an uncoiling spring. He struggled to force movement into his cramped limbs, battling desperately on the slippery surface to avoid following Linus Kypp over edge, but somehow his boots found a patch of stable surface and he stilled himself, panting with relief.

Suddenly he became aware of Silas Glaswall pacing towards him, thumbing back the hammer of his pistol. Glaswall, his narrow, mean face contorted, his blood-shot eyes glinting and crazy.

'No need to worry, Angus Troon,' he grated out. 'I'll be dumping your body over that cliff anyway. Just as soon as I put a bullet in you. If that don't kill you, I guess you'll be as dead as old Linus when you hit the bottom.'

Angus ground his teeth. Sprawled on the ground as helpless as a swatted fly, death loomed before him. But there were still things he had to find out.

'Who raped my wife, Glaswall?'

Glaswall aligned his pistol with Angus's chest, his lips widening into a death-mask grimace.

'Well, I'll put your mind at rest, Mister Ferryman,' he said. 'I can tell you that I sampled the delights of Leah Troon's sweet body — and I bet, while she'd never admit it, she loved every moment of it! She bit a chunk out my tongue, mind. Still hurts like hell.'

'And Johnny Kypp?' Angus persisted, spitting the words out through teeth clenched with hatred.

'Johnny? He never had no designs on her. Johnny went soft after he trashed that vegetable garden. Went back on his word, wouldn't help kill them hosses, betrayed Duquemain and betrayed me. I'll see he pays for that after I've finished with you.'

'Arabella had a different story,' Angus countered. 'She reckoned Johnny raped her, the same as he did my Leah.'

Glaswall shook his head. It was growing colder and he was getting impatient.

'Ain't no time for conversation,' he said. 'But I can tell you that Arabella was real sweet on Johnny, but he didn't want nothin' to do with her. He reckoned she was poison. So I guess she figured she'd get her own back on him by spreading them lies.'

Anguish was rising in Angus like a tidal wave, anguish that death would prevent him from effecting retribution on this evil man.

Glaswall turned to spit, then swung back towards his victim. 'Goodbye, Mister Ferryman.'

He fired, but Angus had lunged to the side. As the lead ploughed past his ear, his hands closed over Linus Kypp's buffalo gun, lying in the snow where the old man had discarded it. Glaswall was thumbing back the hammer for his second shot, when Angus swung the muzzle of the big weapon in the outlaw's direction and pulled the trigger. The gun exploded, a thunderous, ear-splitting roar.

It was not an accurate shot. It did not blow Glaswall's head from his shoulders as intended. Instead, the heavy lead drove into his chest, hurling him back and down. But amazingly he staggered to his feet. Somehow, he raised his pistol again, but he never pressed the trigger. The weapon slipped from his grasp. His eyes flickered. His hands flailed, both fists clutched beneath his breast bone. Blue, bubbling foam drooled from the edges of his mouth. Slowly, he sank to his knees, panting for air, instinctively trying to cover the big, bloody spout pumping through the gaping hole in his coat. He reeled back, gazed at Angus for a second with incredulity stamped across his narrow face, then he plunged forward into the snow. Twice, his body quivered in its death throes. Then it became still.

Angus stumbled to him, hooked his boot beneath his belly and heaved him on to his back. Glaswall was a gory mess. He stooped over him, seeking any faint sign of life that he could club out, finding none. Instead, the smell of the man seeped into his nostrils

— onions and whiskey.

He stepped back and spoke four words. *That was for Leah!*

Afterwards he cut Otto Kruger free. The German was weak from loss of blood, only semi-conscious — but somehow he would survive the journey back to civilization and medical care. Angus would ensure that.

21

'I hear,' Elizabeth said, a little coyly, making out it was fresh news to her, 'that you're buying back the ferry. Rebuilding it.'

It was a month later and they were in the livery.

He paused as he groomed Judas.

Working from a pail of water, Elizabeth was sponging the bullet-gash along the sorrel's flank. It was healing well. Edmund Clayton had shown himself good at treating horses as well as humans. And his daughter had proved a caring veterinary nurse.

Angus looked at Elizabeth, noticing, for the first time, how her blue-grey eyes were luminous, like the early morning sky.

'Ay,' he nodded. 'I've handed in my deputy's badge and spoken to Kruger. He's only too happy to get his money back. When he gets over his wounds, he'll make a fresh start some place else.'

Angus didn't mention that he was also giving the German his reward money for killing Glaswall.

For a moment his mind drifted to Johnny Kypp. He was amazed at the way he had been cut up over his father's death. You would have thought he and old Linus had been bosom pals. Angus realized that all his suspicions, or at least most of them, over Johnny's motives had been ill-founded. The former outlaw now seemed to be taking his duties as town marshal positively to heart, having cast aside his previous criminality.

Angus could see how Elizabeth was anxious to say something and was struggling to find the right words.

'If you're rebuilding the house, Angus,' she eventually said, 'maybe I could help you. I'd like that. I'm a good worker, you know.'

'Elizabeth, I know that,' he admitted,

'but things could never be the same. Without Leah, I mean.'

She nodded. She was looking sad and intensely serious. 'I realize things could never be the same. I could never take her place. But I just had this idea that I could help in some way.'

'You're only seventeen,' he said.

'Eighteen last week,' she argued. 'And there's something else.' A glint of anger flared in her eyes. Defiantly she said: 'I love you, Angus.'

'How can you be sure?' he asked.

'Love is like the wind,' she answered. 'You can't see it, but you can feel it certain as anything. I *know* it's there.'

He laughed and realized it was the first time he had done so since Leah's death. It was if a deadening callus had been lifted from him. 'You're a funny lass,' he said.

And then, very gently, he took her in his arms and kissed her, and she was trembling with all the pent-up emotion she'd displayed that night at Kelly's Hole.

He whispered her name and instinctively she knew that she was victorious, and that he was giving her the assurance she craved.

THE END

CHEYENNE GALLOWS

Tyler Hatch

Digging gold in Sonora they had outsmarted the claim-jumpers. Now they aimed to buy the biggest Texan horse ranch this side of the Great Divide. But they stopped at Buckeye, and Nolan met Abby Lightfoot — half-blooded Sioux, and full-blooded woman . . . Then the big trouble started. It would end hundreds of miles north, where Custer's shadow still lurked and hatred for the white man was part of life. Guns had started the feud and guns would finish it.

IRON EYES MUST DIE

Rory Black

Bounty hunter Iron Eyes had tracked down his prey to an hotel at Rio Concho. He quickly despatches them and, with the hotel ablaze, drags the bodies outside. But waiting for him is Sheriff Brook Payne and his deputies with rifles trained on him. Iron Eyes is charged with murder and thrown in jail to be tried as soon as Judge Franklin Travis, better known as the Hanging Judge, arrives in town. Can Iron Eyes escape the noose?

THE CHOSEN GUN

Chad Hammer

So far as Chade Stocker was concerned when Capital City hired his gun, it was just another heat-blasted town down on its luck and in need of a little Colt .45 peacemaking. He showed no mercy for any of the outlaw gangs, or the wild women, or the desperadoes they sent to kill him. It was only when young Jesse McKidd rode in to face Stocker down that the county would know which man was indeed the chosen gun.

OUTLAW VENGEANCE

Greg Mitchell

Scout Jeff Malone and his patrol have Jonas Grigg captured and his gang cornered. Concerned over potential casualties from the cross-fire, Malone strikes a deal with the outlaw, allowing him a peaceable departure. But, once free, a humiliated Grigg swears revenge . . . Tracing Malone to Rocky Creek, he plans to kill his adversary and rob the town bank. Ominously, mysterious gunmen appear and an acquaintance of Malone is murdered. Can Malone ever hope to destroy the threat of the outlaw's vengeance?